Chilly Little Thing
Sonya Lawson

SauceBox Press

Copyright © 2024 by Sonya Lawson

All rights reserved.

No portion of this book may be reproduced in any form without written permission from the publisher or author, except as permitted by U.S. copyright law.

To all those needing some easy fluffiness in their lives right now.
I feel you and I hope this helps, even if only for a short time.

This book contains scenes that may depict, mention, or discuss: light bullying, cheating (but not with the main couple), and harassment by an ex. Please take care of yourself as you read.

Contents

Chapter 1	1
Chapter 2	12
Chapter 3	29
Chapter 4	34
Chapter 5	43
Chapter 6	53
Chapter 7	62
Chapter 8	73
Chapter 9	86
Chapter 10	95
Chapter 11	104
Chapter 12	113
Chapter 13	121
Chapter 14	133
Chapter 15	148
Chapter 16	160

Chapter 17	169
Chapter 18	179
Want More?	187
About the Author	188
Acknowledgements	189

Chapter 1

Most people didn't have to obsess over Christmas candles, but Lily wasn't one of those people.

On this afternoon in late November, she took a huge bite of her turkey and cheddar sandwich as she stared at her laptop, flipping through her Etsy site, tweaking things as she went. She needed to add a new Christmas candle before the week ended, but she actually didn't have one yet. Not the candle. Not even the formula. Her creativity had stalled out on her. So she chewed slowly, piddled on her laptop, and half-stared into space while she was supposedly on lunch. She got no actual lunch break because on weekdays she worked alone until her high school student employee came breezing in after classes. Instead, she did what she did most days: ate her homemade sandwich and napkin full of potato chips at the counter, ready to sock it away in case anyone came in to buy something.

Not a great idea to take such big old bites in this scenario, though, because she nearly choked when the tiny golden bell above her door chimed, alerting her to a potential customer. She managed to swallow the momentarily lodged chunk of food. When she looked up with only a rim of tears in her eyes from the ordeal, she eased back in her stool a bit while giving a happy wave to her shop neighbor.

Betty Booth and her husband Ralph owned the bakery next door and had for a good fifty years. The older woman shuffled forward slowly, a broad smile on her deeply wrinkled face even as her back stooped slightly. "Workin' hard or hardly workin'?" she called mid-shuffle and cackled at her own joke. A joke she used at least once a week but one Lily still found amusing.

"Just lost in my thoughts. How's your day been?"

"Lordy, long. These feet can't hold up like they used to." Lily jumped up to bring her stool around the counter for Betty at her words, but the older woman shooed her away. "No need, but I thank ya. Not staying long. Just came by to drop off one of these before we close up shop."

"Already sold out?" Betty and Ralph made a finite amount of cookies, donuts, and pastries every day, and the shop closed promptly whenever they sold out. Somehow, even in their small Appalachian town, it usually happened around lunchtime, especially when everyone craved a tasty Christmas cookie.

Betty nodded as a gentle yet satisfied smile stretched across her deep mauve painted lips. "Always the way of it come Christmas time. We make more now, but still run out right quick."

Lily nodded. She usually sold more, in person and online, come Christmastime, too. Partly because Holly Hollow, the tiny Eastern Kentucky town where they lived, decided to run with their name and make it a cute Christmas shopping destination filled with artisan storefronts in a retro downtown area. "Downtown" consisted of a strip of cute shops about four blocks long, so not huge or anything, but filled with character, especially at Christmastime.

To be honest, she'd sold a good bit this holiday season, but not nearly as much as last year. Her online sales had taken a big dive. COVID created a lot of business havoc, but it'd made her go online and brought her a good bit of new income in the past four years. Except for this year for some reason.

No, if Lily were honest with herself, sales dipped because of her lack of inspiration. She'd become known for new, innovative candle scents using unlikely combinations of local, fresh ingredients. This year, for some reason, come October, she just couldn't get it together. The creative juices weren't flowing. Now she stared December full in the face and she had no new Christmas candle. Not good.

"Anyways, love, wanted you to try this one." Betty thrust a waxy white bag toward Lily, shaking it when she didn't automatically grab for it.

Lily opened the crinkly paper to find a lovely Linzer cookie, star shaped, with a star cut out in the middle, red jam peeking through the sprinkling of powdered sugar. She held it up in her hand, admiring the art of it as the smell of berry goodness hit her full force. Her sandwich long forgotten in the face of a delicious Betty cookie, she took a bite as the old woman watched with a smirk on her face. Bright, deep fruity flavor burst on her tongue and buttery cookie snapped back, mellowing the tart with sweetness.

"Dang it, Betty." she managed to say after the first bite. "That's awfully good. What's that jam? I get cranberry, but also something else."

"Wild blackberry, handpicked in the deep woods and jammed this summer."

"You have more energy than me," Lily said in wonder at all Betty still did at 70-plus years old.

"Ppsshh, child. You just need a reason to get up and go." She stopped and looked around the shop a moment before adding, "Found 'em just on the edge of the national forest, deep in a hollow about a mile out from a gravel road Ralph likes to wander. I'll write out more directions for you real quick." Betty swiped a piece of paper from the counter and a pen from Lily's holder and started scribbling as she talked about turning down this road and driving past this landmark and so on. She pushed the directions at Lily. "You go have a look this weekend. Kickstart your brain a bit."

Apparently Betty also knew things weren't too hot with her this holiday season. Not like it wasn't obvious, when her shop bell wasn't ring-a-linging too often and her delivery pick-ups hadn't picked up.

"Except, maybe you shouldn't head out there today, what with dark coming on so early this time a year. Been hearing odd things of late about the deep forest."

"Oh yeah?" Lily asked, only half paying attention because she focused on another bite of the beautiful cookie in her hands.

"People talk about seeing a white bear in the woods."

The oddity of that statement forced her attention away from the cookie. "White bear?" Brown bear, sure. They'd been more abundant in recent years. "You mean like a polar bear?"

Betty raised her hands and shook her head. "I ain't seen nothing, mind, but like I said, people talk, and a few have said they've seen a big, hulking white beast when they got a little too deep in them woods."

Hard to believe, seeing as polar bears were exclusive to the arctic, but Lily shrugged at the information. There were a lot of things stalking the deep dark of Appalachia, and anyone from there could tell their own stories about strange things they saw or heard when out and about in the forests.

"Could it be a werewolf?"

"Doubt it. They're territorial, and their territories never stretched this far east or north for the Kentucky or Tennessee packs."

Lily nodded in agreement. Of all the facts people knew of werewolves, which wasn't much given the history of humans and supernaturals, one of the two constants was that werewolves ran in packs in specific territories they maintained and stuck to without fail. Could one wander? She supposed. But also seemed just as likely some other, unknown creature roamed there. Lily felt certain there had to be more in this world than what people already knew.

"Welp," the woman said, clapping her hands together on a sharp crack, causing Lily to jump out of her internal thoughts of supernaturals and Appalachian mysteries. "Heading out now. Me and Ralph need to close down and go on home."

"Thanks for the treat, Betty," Lily called as the woman shuffled away. She waved her thanks off as she shuffled back out the door as the mailman, Jed, held the door open for her.

"Deliveries, Lily?" He asked after Betty cleared the way and he placed her mail on the counter.

"Yep. A few at least. One sec." Lily left her lunch, and the beautiful cookie, on her counter and made her own shuffle back to grab the few deliveries she had for the day. Not much, but at least it was something.

"LILY!" Isa screamed, in that way only teenage girls can—shrill and loud and so very effective.

She took the time to run her hands under water and scrub hard, though not for the full recommended 20 seconds. She didn't want the yell to come again. Drying her hands on a tea towel as she hurried out of the back room she called her lab, Lily surveyed the scene.

Her candle shop was bright and airy and minimal, even with the Christmas decorations now trimming the place. She'd gone with a Scandinavian design vibe when she opened a few years ago: white walls, bright and shiny pine floors and shelves, and white-cloth draped tables with enough space between them to move comfortably and experience the scents. With something like a candle shop, Lily figured you needed space to really make sure the smells mingled as little as possible.

For the season, sprigs of fresh holly and pinecones from the surrounding forests were added, along with big loops of twinkling white lights where wall met ceiling. A few pops of red velvet ribbon here and there added color. It appeared clean, fresh, and festive all at once, something she thought of as a brand of sorts for Lily's Lights.

Right then, standing in the middle of all the minimalistic good-time Christmas vibes with the perfect mix of teenage indifference and dismissal on her face, Isa stared down Madison.

Lily gave an inward groan at the sight. Not at Isa. She loved her. Isa worked part time. She came in for a few hours after school three days a week and all day on Saturdays. She was kind, smart, liked to keep busy, and made good sales.

No, the issue was Madison. Honestly, Lily's thoughts on the woman waffled far too often. She thanked the Christmas spirits the woman had taken over bookkeeping for her a few years ago because Lily hated math in all forms. Having Madison take it on was a godsend for her tension headaches. Dealing with Madison's sometimes snooty attitude and gossipy ways, however, tested her at the best of times. Isa had zero patience for the lady, regardless of her connection to the shop, and let her lack of patience be known without fail. Hence the stare down.

"Hey there, Madison. What's up?"

"Hi, Lily. Kinda dead in here, right?"

Lily gritted her teeth at the dig, but carried on. "Need something?"

"Yeah," she said, digging into the massive Micheal Kors tote hanging from her left shoulder. She pulled out a printed sheet of paper. "In the new year, I'm switching over to different software. I'll need you to connect your POS with it so I can pull all your info when needed. Here's the instructions."

"Sure thing," Lily said, looking over the paper Madison handed her quickly to see they didn't seem too complicated.

"Shouldn't be a problem for you," Madison said with a sniff. "Speaking of, you seen the Booths? They ain't never open."

Isa sneered and looked about to say something, so Lily jumped in quick to save them the hassle of a snipe fest between Isa and Madison. "They sold out early again. They'll be at home, though. You can stop by there. Or, if you like, I'll drop a copy to them tomorrow morning."

Madison waved a hand in the air. "Don't bother. They'll need to be talked to. I guess I'll just come by earlier tomorrow." She took Lily in for a minute, giving her a solid up and down. Lily knew what she saw. The ankle-length beige shirt dress with the denim apron she and Isa both wore as a sort of shop uniform hugged her soft body nicely but was likely wrinkled this late in the day. The comfy and practical—meaning not too pretty—brown leather flats she wore didn't add pizzazz to her outfit. Her thin, brown hair always started neat in her bob in the mornings, but throughout the day it turned a little more and more disheveled, no matter what she tried to do with it. Her face was pale, round, with a matching round button nose, topped with a bright dimpled smile and round, gray eyes the color of winter clouds. All and all, nothing to sneeze at in Lily's own estimation, but Madison always found fault wherever she looked, be it at Lily or around the shop, where she focused her eyes next.

"No new scent this season?" The question held hints of curiosity and accusation, something Lily didn't want to deal with right then.

"Nope. Not yet."

"Little late," Madison muttered as her shiny, pointed-toe black boots tapped against the blonde wood floors.

"I have plans," Lily said, then latched onto Betty's plan for good measure. "About to go out this weekend to gather some new ingredients."

"Hmm," Madison hummed, as if she didn't exactly believe her.

Isa sucked in a breath and Lily knew full well if she started, Madison would get an ear full of teenage girl tirade, so she patted her arm to stop her before she let loose.

"Very well. Let me know when you have new stock. And be mindful out there. Been word of bears and such around. Maybe don't go out alone." That right there kept Lily from fully disliking Madison. She came off as snooty, judgy, and a little too big for her britches, but she could also be considerate at surprising times. Glimmers of what Madison could be if she let go of the judgement.

Lily also thought it odd that twice in one day people came in her shop talking bears, but she pushed it aside. Any worry of bears paled next to her worry for making her holiday sales a success. "Anything else going on?"

"Nope," Madison said, her word popping before her smile turned a little sharp. "Saw Ryan today. Just added him as a client, in fact."

Lily's body locked at that bit of info, more so than any talk of bears. Ryan was her ex. Her one serious ex-boyfriend. They'd dated in high school and through most of college. He went off to law school in Lexington when they were both in their mid-twenties. She had dreams of marriage and babies. One day she decided to surprise him. Surprise him she did, because she caught him in bed with someone else.

She'd said nothing, simply walked out the door and out of Ryan's life. He'd harassed her for a bit, pleading for another chance before his words turned sharp and ugly. It got bad enough, with the insistent calls and following her around and cornering her in public, that her older brother Michael stepped in and made him stop after threatening him with a beating. She hadn't needed her brother's brand of help in the seven years since, but Michael worked on an oil rig in the Gulf now, and she didn't need the problem of Ryan again. She just hoped he was over it all, like her. Or as much as a woman could be after something like that happened. Her heart didn't ache any longer, but it was shaped different now for sure.

"He came back here?"

"Yep," Madison said with another annoying pop. "Sure did. Set up a law office right down the street there. Doing estate and probate stuff. I'm sure you'll see him around."

"Sure," Lily said, but added nothing else, making her face morph into her bland sales smile. Madison stared back, but when Lily didn't participate further, or give her more ammo to talk about with others, she shrugged.

"Okay then. See you around, Lily. Isa."

Isa gave a huff in response but Madison had already turned her back, click-clacking on heeled boots out the door.

"That lady," Isa gritted out.

"Helps me out a lot," Lily finished.

"Still. Why's she gotta be so hateful? Talking about Betty and Ralph in that tone when they're sweet as pie. Bringing up Ryan to you. She's a bitch."

"Hush," Lily said, but the laugh in her voice betrayed her true thoughts. "She does us a service."

"Which you pay her to do. You don't pay her to give her mouth."

"True," Lily whispered then sighed. "Everything good out here?"

"Yeah, sure. Slow, but fine."

Slow wasn't good this time of year. It needed to pick up more, which meant she needed to get her butt back in the lab. "I'll be in the back, yeah?"

Isa nodded and fussed with the center display of basic pine-scented candles. Lily moved to the back to try to come up with new inspiration, thoughts of Christmas candles, new software, holiday shopping season, exes and bears crowding her mind.

Chapter 2

Several days later, Lily spent her Saturday night as she usually did: with a glass of wine in hand and a fantasy show on tv. Sure, she occasionally went out with friends, but she didn't have too many of those. Not because she wasn't liked or didn't like people, she was just a bit of an introvert. She enjoyed solitude or easy companionship and lived her life accordingly.

The drink, crackling fire, and show worked well for her on this cold Saturday night. This one included a werewolf and witch romance. A bit of a stretch, as every human knew supernatural beings almost always stuck to their own, but that's what tv was for, right? To add a little romantic fantasy to the world, make it all look and feel so easy, when romance was anything but.

Humans knew little of werewolves or witches or vampires, to be honest. And for good reason; history books were littered with the horrible things people did to supernaturals when they decided to expose themselves and tried to live alongside, if not among, humans centuries ago. Werewolf hunts, vampire stakings, witch burnings. Bad, bad things, all in the name of fearing some new monster. It was often the way with people, Lily thought with more than a touch of sadness. They hurt what they don't understand.

Now, however, things were different. More progressive and far less bloody. Supernaturals kept to themselves, sure, but there weren't all out wars against them perpetrated by humans. In some cities, supernaturals and humans even lived side by side, or at least vampires and witches did. Still, in small towns like hers, the supernatural beings of the world usually didn't stick around if or when they showed up for any reason.

The forests of Appalachia, however, were vast and held many secrets. Maybe there was a supernatural man out there for her with a strong body, rough voice, and kind soul who'd sweep her off her feet like no human man had done in her over three decades of life. She snorted at the absurdity of the idea, even as a not so small part of her wished it might come to pass during some solo walk in the woods. The silly romance show, which she loved, got to her head sometimes, but it was a good thing she could think on something different for a spell.

After the week she had, the distraction of wine and story and random romantic daydreams eased the tension. Madison's software conversion proved more difficult than she thought, which went double for Betty and Ralph, who she helped through the process, as Madison liked to talk down to the older couple and Lily liked to spare them from it where and when she could. She had a notion to give the woman piece of her mind about customer service, but all of them needed her on some level, and they all also knew her. How she acted.

Isa had been at choral rehearsals for their Christmas performance most nights that week. Lily happily cheered her on when she discussed it, would cheer even louder when she went to the show, but Isa being busy left her short-handed in the store. Sadly, she could handle it because it just wasn't as busy as it should be. Which is why she sat alone, with wine and TV, worrying.

As more delicious supernatural romance picked up on the screen, her mind drifted to what she would do. What she needed to do. The week past had gone about the same as it had all season: a steady influx of in-person and online sales, but nothing at all like her Christmas season usually went. As this sales period usually made up the bulk of her annual revenue, she worried. She'd had grand plans: her own website sales, a wider national reach for her products, and more people to help her out so she wouldn't be so damn tired come Saturday nights. If she didn't do something, and soon, those ideas would fizzle and die. She'd survive, sure, but it'd be a lot of scrimping and saving and casting her hopes aside for at least another year or two. The years stacked up quick when people hit their thirties, and Lily didn't want to see them dissolve like the first winter snow, leaving dingy, disappointed dreams in their wake.

Equally disappointing in the day to day was the look on her customers' faces when they discovered she didn't have a new candle for Christmas. She'd become known and she wanted to deliver what they expected from her, for them and their Christmas hopes as well as for her own pride. Dreams and pride so often mingled together, and Lily didn't want to prick either one of them.

Sadly, all her ideas misfired. Call it her inspiration, lighting, muse, whatever. She'd lost the thing that gave her products their unique spark. Lily had spent weeks now in her little lab, mixing new scents and ingredients, but nothing hit right for this season. She'd found some interesting combos for other candles, but nothing rang in the Christmas spirit just yet.

She shook her head to clear it and focus back on her tv. She needed a break. Something outside herself to jump start her creativity. Betty'd given her solid directions to her blackberry patch in the deep forest. Lily hadn't ever gone in that far. One, she didn't want to unknowingly get into the national forest and come afoul of some ranger who wouldn't appreciate her picking things. Or inadvertently wander onto someone's patch of land and get called out as a poacher, or worse. People didn't take kindly to trespassers around here.

Betty'd told her it'd be easy. She'd had no problems, and if a seventy-three-year-old woman could wander around that hollow, by God she could too.

A different scene, different ingredients. Those might do it for her. At least, she hoped it would.

The internal circles she walked herself around were interrupted not by the show on her screen, but the shrill sound of her phone. Her landline in fact, the one she kept for emergencies as her grandma always taught her. She'd not used the thing in ages. Hadn't heard it ring in twice as long. The sound rang clear and loud from the old-school housing and twirly cord blaring from her kitchen wall.

She rose from her couch, a straight, open view of the kitchen before her interrupted by a small wall with her TV above a wood-burning fireplace insert. Skirting the short wall and crackling fire, wineglass sloshing slightly at her double-step, she moved around the head of her small kitchen table and over to the black, vintage phone she paid maybe a little too much for on Amazon. It looked so much like the one she'd grown up with she'd just had to have it, a small black box with the earpiece nestled in a hanging slot. The weight gave an odd reassurance as she wrapped her fingers around the skinny body and brought the big, round earpiece up to the side of her head.

"Hello?" Nothing. No sound there, not even the creepy breathing she'd get if she were in some horror movie.

"Hello?" She asked again, this time an edge of annoyance in her tone. She figured they could say something, at least, even if they dialed the wrong number.

Again, nothing. Then a click, and after a second, dial tone. She moved the handpiece in front of her, stared down at it and muttered "weird" to herself before giving a slight shrug and hanging it back up.

People often changed their cell numbers. Hell, you could even get an internet phone number from the area even if you didn't live there. Could've been anyone, really. Still, something wiggled in the back of her mind, a little piece of something she thought she should remember but couldn't quite reach.

Didn't matter in the moment. She swiped her wineglass back up from where she'd deposited on the kitchen counter, and turned back to her living room. Back to brothers fighting monsters. Hopefully enough of a distraction to clear her head and give her space to think on her forest trip in the morning.

CHILLY LITTLE THING

"At least there ain't snow," Lily spit out from chattering teeth as she picked her way down a steep embankment. The woods were thick there, dark and deep, and she marveled again at the idea of Betty getting herself down here.

She'd followed the directions to the T. Or, as to the T as she could when Betty'd written down things like "Hook a right at the stump that looks like a bench seat and stay going north until you find the big old fallen pine on your left."

"Shit," she yelped, as her foot slipped on the icy dew still covering the untouched forest floor and she stumbled down a few steps before righting herself by grabbing onto a sturdy but thin birch tree. Her nerves calmed with a few deep breaths, and she kept going, her big gathering basket, the same one she'd used with her granny when they went foraging together decades ago, dangling from the crook of her left elbow.

Eventually, she made her way down into the bottom of the small hollow. The ridge line loomed above, large enough to keep the low-lying winter sun from making an appearance at the bottom. Lily let out a gust of breath thinking about how much she didn't want to climb back up to the top, but it was what it was. Nothing for it at the moment.

She turned in a circle, looking at the strip of lowland littered with branches, leaves, and other frosted forest debris. Down a good bit she saw the brambles where Betty must've picked those blackberries. A small creek-bed meandered off to the left but the little running water barely bubbled and Lily figured it was most likely frozen. Frozen as she felt, despite bundling up in sweats, a puffy down coat, and the thick wool gloves and beanie Sarah, the owner of the knitting shop a few spaces down from her candle store, made for her a few Christmases ago. Lily blew into her hands now cupped over her face, partially to warm the wool and partially to warm up her nose. It was colder than a witch's tit out there, so she needed to be about her business.

She moved closer to the creek bed, exploring with her eyes and a few nudges of her hiking-boot clad feet. Twigs, rocks, small bones, mud. That was all she really found under the leaves there. Made sense, as not much could grow in a hollow this dark, but she'd come to find some inspiration and she'd be damned if she left emptyhanded.

Then, something across the way caught her eye. A lump of a plant, no longer in leaf but still intact enough to show the distinct heart-shaped leaves of wild ginger. Her mind spun.

Wild ginger. Mace. Molasses. Nutmeg. Warm ginger cookies.

A wide smile broke across her cold face as she moved toward the ginger. Just what she needed. One of the only reasons she'd never done ginger before was because there were laws about how much you could harvest based on the size and age of plants, and ginger poaching caused a whole lot of problems. The plant across the creekbed looked safe to harvest without any worries, a rare find for sure.

Without much in her head beyond candle scents and packaging, she moved to jump over the small creek bed. A normal feat at the best of times, but she should've thought of the frosty dew and the frozen water. She didn't. Lily cleared the edge easy enough, but soon discovered the slick remnants of frost, which didn't give her much traction. For a moment, she thought she'd made it. She caught herself on her second foot when the first slipped, but it wasn't quick enough. Her ankle bent odd, twisting right out from under her. With a cry, she went down to one knee, then rolled onto her butt to check the damage. She rolled her ankle in a circle, wincing as it stretched. Not broken, so some good news. She'd twisted it for sure, but hopefully not much.

Wild ginger now forgotten, she threw her head back and screamed, letting her pent-up frustration at her shit luck release with the sound. She'd had a time of it lately, and this may well be the straw that broke her back. The pain in her ankle meant she'd have a hell of a time getting herself out of the hollow.

Of course, her cell didn't work. Hadn't had service for a good bit out in these woods. Nothing for her to do but attempt to claw her way out on her own.

Gritting her teeth, she went up to her knees, breathing in and out to prepare herself to take on her weight. She'd find a big stick or something to help get up the embankment, but she'd have to get on her feet first.

However, before she could get to her feet, she heard a distinct sound from the edges of the dark woods in front of her. The sound of a large thing letting out a huff of air. A thing like a bear. She'd dismissed the stories of white bears from earlier in the week, now the idea made her freeze. There may be bears in these woods, but white or black, they shouldn't be out and about in winter. If it was a bear in winter, that meant real bad things. They'd have woken from hibernation for some reason and wouldn't be happy about it.

Could be anything, or at least, that's what her brain told her.

Other beings walked this earth; she knew that much in her bones as a good daughter of Appalachia. Never whistle in the woods. Never answer to your name being called in the night. And, apparently, never go to a winter hollow alone, early on a Sunday morning.

A shuffling sound reached her next, and the hair on her arms stood up under all her layers. That was most definitely the sound of something's feet moving through dead leaves.

"Hello?" she croaked out, much less assured than when she'd asked the phone the same question the night before.

Stillness, another huff, then a deep, gruff voice. "Do you require help?" The question sounded nice enough, though she detected a definite note of aggravation in the voice. His voice. Sounded like a man for sure. Which, to be honest, didn't exactly make her feel any better. What was some dude doing out there all quiet and hidden while she stumbled around the hollow?

She thought about it. Maybe a little too long, because she heard shuffling feet again. Afraid to be left injured and alone, she made her mind up real quick. "Yes. Please."

A deep sigh drifted from the forest, along with a word muttered under his breath in a way she knew it was a cuss word even if she didn't recognize the language. "Okay. Okay. I suppose..." Nothing else came from the man for a few heavy beats until he said, "Do not be alarmed. I am simply going to help you. Nothing else. Yes?"

"Okay?" She didn't sound so sure, but what else could she do? Why warn her like this? Maybe the bear would have been a better choice?

"Fine." Silence for a beat then, "Try not to scream."

She jolted at those words, which meant her body locked up when he stepped from the shadows and she understood why he'd said what he did.

He towered tall, well over six and a half feet. As she looked up, up, up his body, which was clad in a toga, of all things, she noted the devastating beauty of his bronzed chest and face. Deep muscles showed to full effect in the little he wore. He sported cut cheekbones, a strong and straight nose, and ice blue eyes. White brows topped them, and a leather band pushed back long, thick winter-white hair from his gorgeous face. His lips were full, though pursed in a hard line. Those lips looked a bit odd, as if they stretched over something more in his mouth, but the hard clinch of his jaw was her immediate concern. It signaled loud and clear he was unhappy about something here.

Even with the sign of annoyance, she saw nothing to outright fear at first, or at least nothing more than any large man. Then she noted the claw-tipped, overlong fingers on his massive hands. The bare, claw-tipped toes of his massive feet digging into the cold earth. The white-feathered wings at his back. And a flash of wicked sharp teeth when he opened his mouth. Explained the shape of his lips she noted moments before, but this knowledge wasn't comforting. For a split second, he looked shocked, fanged mouth hanging open for a beat and icy eyes wide, but his face smoothed over quickly, surprise replaced with determined concentration.

She bit back a yelp of surprise and tried to school her own face, which was likely bug-eyed. She needed help, he'd offered, and the little experience she did have with the occasional supernatural in her store eased her mind after the initial shock. They were all living on this planet, if not all humans, and what she knew from popular media and limited interactions said they were all more alike than not. She was no supernatural bigot. The man in front of her might not be human, but she could give him the same benefit of the doubt she'd give a human man in the woods. Which was, admittedly, not much benefit and more than a little doubt. That is, until he spoke again.

"As I said, I will not hurt you."

All she could do was nod, unable to speak after the way his words landed a soft blow to her gut. Not from the words themselves, but the sound of his voice registering somewhere in the dark recesses of her brain. Lily knew she should be nervous, should experience the cold tendrils of fear or at least hesitation because they were alone out there together. Except her gut told her he didn't lie, so it wasn't really fear making her freeze in his presence. Actually, her gut tugged towards him, and a small but persistent word echoed in her mind: *MINE*. The absurdity of it made her shake her head, to dislodge the odd word, but it stayed stuck right there.

He moved closer, and the hit to her gut tightened into something low and pleasant and unknown. His jaw tightened as if he gritted back something but he continued on with cautious movements, the way someone might approach an injured animal in the woods.

When he crept close enough to kneel beside her, a frown pushed his white eyebrows into a deep, wrinkled V. "What happened?"

After a few failed attempts to vocalize something without "mine" trying to push its way free, she finally got out, "Twisted my ankle." She held it up in the air like a toddler demanding someone tie her shoe. Ridiculous, but what else could she do? He appeared to be a supernatural of some sort, like nothing she'd seen before, but she felt a comfort with him from deep in her gut. She'd been taught to trust her gut, in life and business, and it'd never steered her wrong before, so she went with it.

He knelt there in the frozen dew, cocking his head in a way she'd seen birds of prey do on nature documentaries, studying the ankle she wiggled at him. "May I?" he asked, gesturing with a claw at her leg.

She nodded as he reached a long, strong arm out and oh so gently gripped her calf. Even through the sweatpants, his fingers seared into her skin, hot and strong on her flesh. Need for him welled up suddenly and inexplicably. Like nothing she'd felt before, with any man, let alone one she just met in the deep woods. She shuddered, trying to push down the moan she wanted to let rip at his touch, and he whipped his head to her, too fast for a person, staring for a moment into her eyes. His icy blues didn't blink, didn't waver, but his nose quivered as he took deep breaths in and out. As if steadying himself, finding his calm. Or scenting her.

Finally, he turned back to her foot, and a wave of disappointment washed over Lily for no reason she could explain. She was all feelings without reason, but she trusted herself enough, to go with it.

One clawed finger slowly exposed her ankle from beneath sweats and thick hiking socks. "Does this hurt?" he asked, his deep voice filled with more gravel than before. He slowly rotated her ankle, and she winced at one point, answering his question.

He lowered her leg, putting his hands on his massive, muscled thighs. He shook his head, and a sigh left his chest. "I might need to carry you out."

Lily's breath caught. This beautiful man, carrying her around the woods. Those strong arms around her, those wicked sharp claws so close. Her heart raced, but not from fear. She'd thought her secret desire from the last night too absurd, but it had become fact, at least in her mind. Quickly and irrevocably. "Very well," she said, as if she were some snooty princess and he was a servant. She internally cursed herself but didn't say more; she couldn't trust herself.

A gasp bubbled up from her, more sensual than surprised, when he scooped her into those strong arms with ease and hefted her up to his chest. Something rumbled there, a growl so primal she shivered in anticipation. Lily looked up into his face, her mouth slightly open. His was, too, his fangs exposed. A swirl of visible breath mingled between them, stretched like slowed time, like the thing in her gut she felt lock into place when he stepped toward her. Like he was hers. And she was his.

He broke eye contact first, turning his head to the side and giving a vicious snarl. It didn't frighten her, but it was enough to break whatever mood had fallen between them, so she turned her head to look ahead as he walked. He somehow knew where she'd been and headed toward the same path she'd taken to get into this whole mess. Strong, silent steps and body heat were all that existed between them for several minutes.

He reached the crest of the hollow in no time at all. Superhuman time, for sure. She'd kept her eyes on the wings over his shoulder—the slight shimmer to the stiff, sharp-looking feathers was mesmerizing—or she might figure he flew up that embankment.

Pausing at the top, just past a tree line, he asked, "How far is your vehicle?"

"Not... not far," she managed. Squirming a bit, she signaled she wanted out of his grip. "You can let me down. The way is flat, and with a stick or something, I can make it back to the road."

He huffed again, gripped her tighter, and stalked on, right for the small, one-lane gravel road about a mile down the way.

"Um, I said I could make it."

"I can reach your vehicle more quickly."

"Sure, but you don't have to."

"I do," he said, the tone so hard she wasn't about to argue with him.

Instead, her Southern hospitality finally kicked back in. "I'm Lily. Nice to meet you. Your name is?"

He hesitated before saying "Boreas."

"Boreas," she repeated, a habit she'd established long ago to remember people's names. He stiffened and started walking even faster than before, the woods blurring around the edges of her sight at their new speed.

"I sure do thank you for the help, Boreas. I was in a bit of trouble there."

"Why were you in the woods alone?"

"Oh, you know. This and that." A ridiculous answer, but she couldn't think all wrapped up in his warmth.

"This and that? This and that?" His repetition got a little harsher each time. "You could have been seriously injured. You should not be in these woods alone."

"Pish-posh. I've walked these woods alone most of my life."

He stared down at her, eyes hard and glittering. "No more."

"Excuse me?"

"No more walking the woods alone."

She almost gave him a piece of her mind when she remembered why she'd been there in the first place and what she'd left behind. "Oh, no," she squealed.

"What?" Boreas held her tight to his chest, his head turning to survey the area for danger.

"I went and hurt my ankle and didn't even get what I wanted. And I left my granny's basket out in the woods." Tears threatened to spill then. The slight pain, the loss of that special piece of her grandmother, the letdown of having a great idea she didn't know if she could now execute. It all fell rather hard on her heart.

"Shush, Lily," Boreas cooed, calming her with his voice and the soft stroke of one sharp claw along her left arm. "All will be well."

She wanted to argue with him, but they were already at her car somehow. He set her on the ground, and she shifted so her right foot took all her weight. "Ice," he demanded as he stared down at her foot.

"Yep. Will do. I think some chill creeped into it and helped. Good thing it's winter, huh?" She opened the car door and turned back to him only to see him several feet away from her, heading back from where they'd came.

She wanted to tell him to stop, to come to her, come with her. Be with her, then and forever if possible. Since those were ridiculous things to say to someone she just met, she instead called out "Hey Boreas?"

He stopped but didn't look back at her. She went on. "Thanks again. You know, if you ever need anything, call me. I'd be happy to help." Lily rattled off her number, but he made no move to save it on a phone or even repeat it back to her. She had no idea if he even had a phone, but didn't everyone these days?

He didn't acknowledge what she said, instead walking away on strong legs at such a steady clip the woods swallowed his massive form in seconds.

Lily let out a sigh of disappointment and longing, then shook the odd thoughts from her head. At least her left ankle was the one hurt. She'd be able to drive home without issue. Then ice it just as Boreas demanded she do. First, of course, now that she had a signal, she fired up her search engine as her car warmed itself. A basic search gave her all she needed to know. Boreas, Greek God of the North Wind, usually depicted as a large white beast of winter. There were no photos of him, because no one knew he existed in real life instead of simply being a myth.

The idea of old gods walking the earth shifted her world view, but only slightly. Knowing about other supernatural beings made the reality jump a little easier. Her own love of stories about supernaturals maybe made Lily herself more apt to both believe and accept. The nature of who she met, the look of him, and the odd wind she'd felt caressing her hurt ankle and keeping it cool added up logically given this new information.

Greek gods walked the earth, even if people forgot; they'd once known this. Hell, the more she thought about it, the more it made sense. Why else would so many stories about these beings trickle down through the centuries if they weren't somehow based in reality?

She laughed to herself over the idea of meeting an actual god out in the woods, though she couldn't shrug off the odd connection and longing she felt for him. Nothing she could do about it, and her ankle was starting to throb. Focusing back on her car, nice and toasty and ready to go, she made a three-point turn in the gravel and headed back home. Where she'd think more of Boreas. Who he was, why he lived in their neck of the woods, the odd yet warm knot in her stomach when he first spoke directly to her, and how safe she'd felt in his arms.

The next morning, Lily woke bright and early to find her granny's basket, filled with wild ginger, sitting on her doorstep. The faint smell of wind and pine lingered, and "mine" hit her lips once again without warning.

Chapter 3

She scurried into work, head down, thoughts of ginger molasses cookies crowding her brain so much her obsessive thoughts of a god were shoved aside. Isa wasn't in until about 4pm, so she had to do things a little differently. As she prepped the store and handled customers, she worked on packaging, creating the labels she'd use. They were beautiful; a stark gold, red, and green plaid background with a bold black serif font reading: A Ginger Christmas. The candle itself would be white, with flecks of gold glitter and small chunks of dried ginger. The mock-up on her computer was gorgeous, and she hoped the product looked as good.

Lily sold and gift-wrapped, completed paperwork and inventory, and wrote out a formula to test later in the day. She also made new pages for the product on her Etsy, but didn't make them live. Not yet. Not until she had something on hand to sell. Her toes tapped to the bluegrass Christmas music softly piped into her storefront, her mood far better than it had been all season.

When Isa breezed in a few minutes before the official start to her shift, Lily spared her a few words then hurried off to her lab. She'd already printed out a handful of the labels, jars were prepped and ready as they always were, and she had a solid formula in hand. Now she needed to make a prototype to ensure it all blended together as she thought it would and the process would be complete.

Her candle creation lab was in a 10x10 storage room she'd converted. She kept stock in what was supposed to be her office, mainly because the temperature control functioned better in there. The lab could get a little warm, especially in the summertime, so it became where she created. She hated paperwork anyway, so she kept most things rolling on the laptop she used while sitting at her shop counter.

In here, she got to do what she loved. Create. She designed the space as a blank canvas, much like the shop itself. Same white walls and pine floors, but with the addition of waist-high pine tables stacked with ingredients. White shelves, constantly stocked with all the bits and bobs for making candles, took over one wall: the rustic ball jars she loved, specially stamped lids with her logo, wicks and wax, and everything else she might need. Beside it, on a small table, sat her fancy-pants printer where she made her own labels for the candles and printed out shipping labels, postcards, and other paper promo products she occasionally used. She went through ink like a squid when she was busy, and she hoped that printer'd be humming soon enough.

A large table the length of the room, held the products cooling and ready to be put into boxes for inventory or shipping. Perpendicular to it stood a smaller table, about six feet long, where she made her prototypes. She placed it close to the door so she could keep a lookout if need be, but when she locked into creative mode, little could drag her away.

She threw her small floral notebook on the table, tightening her slightly loosened denim apron as she did, but her pretty little book slid down the slick pine and bumped up against a different book. One she'd never seen before. It was old, worn leather. As in ancient leather–more ancient than she'd ever held in her hand. The pages appeared yellowed with age and thicker than modern book pages, as if handmade from pulp. Latin spread across the pages, or what she guessed to be Latin from her limited experience in an anatomy class. A hint here and there of something like really old English also popped out at her. An English so old it wasn't even from Shakespeare's time. English old enough only a few words here and there were somewhat recognizable. The cover, however, read all Latin. Bright gilded letters twinkled in the light on the front and spine. The same letters: *Liber Desideriorum*. She pulled out her phone to see what it meant, and to confirm it was Latin. The name made her stomach flutter. *Liber Desideriorum: The Book of Desires*.

The oddest thing, though, was the literal shock she felt when she first picked it up. Not like lightning or static or anything, more like a warm, hard pulse of radiant heat. Surprise at the feeling became confusion when the book flipped open in her hand to a page she couldn't read. It looked similar to a recipe from a cookbook or one of her candle formulas.

"Isa!" Lily yelled out, turning the book over in her hands.

"Yep, boss lady," the teen chirped as she stuck her head in the door.

"This yours?"

Isa shook her head in answer. Weirder and weirder. Lily then remembered the basket of wild ginger on her doorstep. The gust of wind that seemed to magically flip the pages. More importantly, she remembered the wind god she'd met the day before and the way his heat radiated deep into her, and felt at ease all of a sudden.

She might've been creeped out by things left on her doorstep or in her shop or knowing a god traipsed through her life. Instead, her gut clenched and her cheeks heated at the idea. She waved Isa off with a muttered "nevermind" when the girl raised perfectly sculpted, dark eyebrows her way then placed the book securely on the small secondary shelf under her table. Lily had work to do, despite the tingles she got thinking about Boreas and his gifts. Pushing her hair back with a headband she kept in her apron, she rolled up her sleeves and started her Christmas candle for the season. Better late than never, as they say.

Her first trial ended up fabulous. No tweaks to the formula needed. That Monday, she stayed late into the night, making two dozen candles before she left. When she did lock the back door and moved to her car, parked mere feet away in her tiny lot, she felt eyes on her. She circled in the chilly winter darkness, looking for who might be out there in the shadows of the night. It didn't feel good, not like the feeling she had when she thought Boreas left her presents. Lily trusted her gut, so she hurried to her car and hopped in, locking her door before she even started it up. Not waiting for the car to warm up, she booked it home, her shoulders tensed as if she could still feel those not-nice eyes on her in the dark.

Lucky for Lily, she forgot about the odd experience as business picked up. By the end of the week, she'd made dozens upon dozens of her new Christmas season candles and sold every one, either in her shop or online. Jed had been loaded down with boxes when he left her shop on Friday afternoon and looked happy about it. Or at least happy for Lily because of it.

She made candles as quickly as she could, even asking Betty to come in for an hour or two here or there to watch the front so she could make more. She'd sell them as soon as they were done. A Ginger Christmas quickly turned into the most successful Christmas candle by a country mile, and she was ecstatic. Only one thing bugged her: her wild ginger store dwindled every day. She might need to go back. To where she met Boreas. Kill two birds with one stone, so to speak. Grab some more ginger and possibly see the god again. The god whose scent and touch called to her back to him like a dull, persistent ache in her belly.

Chapter 4

She stayed late that Saturday, happy to work into the night to create more candles for shop inventory and ignore the longing growing in her every day. The bulk of what she made were the new Christmas scent, but she had to refill a few of her standbys because when someone bought one candle, they often bought another. Especially when they shopped online. Better to pay for shipping once and all that.

She spread the last of her printed labels on the last of her filled jars, patting it affectionately for good measure, when a cold wind somehow blew through her lab. The sensation wasn't unpleasant. The air moved up her spine like a caress and, with the pleasant chill, it caused a deep shudder to trip over her body, leaving goosebumps in its wake. The smell of pine and winter winds filled the space, despite the mix of so many scents, and she whipped her head to the window, somehow knowing what she'd see before her eyes clapped on Boreas.

He stooped by her backdoor, a basket in his hands heaped high with wild ginger. He'd known her need without even being told. The god stepped back, paused for a second to look over his offering, then turned on his heels so quickly his wings faced her before she registered any movement.

Her heart thumped and a string somewhere in her gut tugged, making her reach up and give three quick knocks on the glass. Boreas stopped, looking over his shoulder to lock icy blue eyes with winter gray ones. Lily smiled brightly at him, held up a finger in the universal sign of "Give me one sec," then hurried as fast as her human feet could move her to the backdoor. Before she opened it, her hand flew up to her head, remembering the tattered old headband she wore. Cursing slightly, she ripped it out of her hair, stuffed it back in her apron, and slicked a hand down her thin, brown bob before heaving out a breath and stepping into the cold night.

There stood the god, in front of her in all his glory once again, the same, or at least a very similar toga draped across his ridiculously wide chest. He stood shoeless on the freezing asphalt of her back lot, the claws on his feet gripping the ground so tight it looked as if he'd leave gouges. His wings shuddered as she opened the door, but he ruffled his feathers and tucked his wings tight to his back. His forearms and biceps, full and bulging, were on full display because he had his arms crossed on his chest, waiting. Why he looked so defensive, she didn't know, but she smiled again to try to put him at ease.

"You must be cold. Wanna come on in?"

"I do not get cold," he said, firm and strong, his delicious voice doing all kinds of things to her insides.

"O-kay," she said after a long pause. "Doesn't answer my question, though. You wanna come in, have some tea with me?"

He stared, icy eyes unwavering, until he slumped slightly forward as if giving up some internal struggle. "Yes." A simple answer, but when he took the first step toward her, relief washed over her.

Lily didn't voice this, however. She simply stepped aside, sweeping her arm into the store in welcome. He stopped right inside the door, his body locking inches from her, his breaths coming in loud, deep pulls.

"The smell can sometimes be overwhelming," she said, referencing the candles, of course, but in the moment, she was overwhelmed by his unique, intoxicating scent. She even swayed slightly toward him, but snapped herself out of it. "Excuse me," she said, grabbing the door to shut it, but finding Boreas's large body in her way.

He side-stepped so she could close the door and lead the way into her small office, where she kept an electric tea kettle. She poured in water from a jug beside her desk left there for this purpose and fired up the thing before moving to the shelf behind her desk to grab two mugs. Lily did all this to calm herself and give herself time to get used to the scent and sensation of him so damn close to her.

When she finished her task and sensed she was a little more in control, she spun to smile up at him. "Please. Have a seat."

His wings rustled as he perched on the edge of the small chair she had in front of her desk. Isa was usually the only one who sat in it. Seeing Boreas in the small white chair, trying to get comfortable with his wings and his bulk, was almost laughable. The unhappy scowl on his face as he maneuvered made her control the laughter.

She busied herself again, steeping tea bags, when she asked over her shoulder, "Sugar? Would offer you milk, but I don't have any."

"No, thank you," he said, all politeness and civility. Lily turned to take her seat and left his cup on the opposite edge of her desk. The small expanse between them, only wood and bits of metal, felt like nothing given the pull in her stomach. A sudden but vivid vision flashed in her mind: Boreas tossing their teas aside, laying her across this desk, and trailing her skin with those sharp claws until she begged him for more.

His nostrils flared, as if he could scent the wetness her vision caused, and Lily blushed. Hell, he was a god, he probably could scent all kinds of things. Something to remember in the future.

"How have you been?" she asked, taking a sip from her too-hot tea but letting the burn focus her attention from her body's reactions to the man. Pleasantries weren't deep or anything, but they were as good a jumping off point as anything else.

"Well. And you?" Boreas also knew niceties then.

"Thankfully busy." Another sip of hot tea, then, "Oh, wait. I forgot I have these."

She grabbed her purse from its handy hook and rummaged in it to find the shortbread Betty'd given her earlier in the day. That woman gave her so many sweets it had to be digging into her profits. Lily complained about it occasionally. Only occasionally, though, because Betty bit her head off any time she did it.

When she opened the small wax bag, the soft scent of orange filled her nose, competing momentarily with the wind and pine.

"Want one?" she asked, offering the buttery, citrusy goodness to the god in front of her.

He cocked his head like a crow studying some new, shiny object, then plucked the offered cookie from between her fingers. When his lips wrapped around the thing, she had to scurry away, albeit a short scurry, to the opposite side of the small room.

"Good, right? The bakery next door keeps me in sweet treats."

"Do you enjoy such things?"

"Of course. Who doesn't? A little sugar makes the world brighter."

"As do candles," the god muttered before putting the final bit of his cookie in his mouth. Lily blushed at the intended compliment. Unsure how to proceed, she took her own bite of orange-y goodness and gave a soft moan at the burst of flavor.

Boreas stood abruptly, the chair bouncing back from the force. "I must go."

She left her seat and hustled around the desk, laying a soft hand on his chest, pleading with her touch. "Why?"

"I came only to help, not to..." he trailed off.

"You did help," she added. "Thank you for bringing me more ginger. I was just thinking I needed to go back out for more."

His chest puffed. "You are not to go to the woods alone again."

Her eyes narrowed in on him. She felt... something with him. She didn't know it, couldn't name it, but it was insanely strong and unwavering. Still, she was no pushover. She'd stopped being that long ago. Wouldn't start up again, even for a god. "I'll do what I need to do to help my business."

He ignored the hard turn of her voice. "Are you in dire straits?"

Lily forehead wrinkled at the question, not quite understanding at first. "Oh, you mean the business? Not exactly. Definitely not anymore, but, you know how it is. With any small business, you've got a razor thin margin of error between making and losing money."

His brows dipped, the deep V they created snagging her interest and mesmerizing her for a minute. So much so she didn't at first hear what he said. "Huh?' she asked, shaking her head to get her focus back on track. To the conversation at hand and not the god's beautiful body hot under her hands.

"I asked if you need assistance."

"Oh, no thank you. I mean, you've already helped an awful lot, what with the ginger and all."

"Do you require more?"

She thought of the basket he'd deposited inside her back door, somehow brimming with wild ginger despite the winter weather and its tendency to wither at the root in the cold. More ginger sat stacked in the hefty basket than she'd ever seen in her life. A possibly illegal amount of ginger, truth be told. "Um, did you take out an entire field of wild ginger?"

He shook his head. "I... I like the smell of ginger. Grow it close. This is but a fraction of what I have spread over the years." They were so close now, his breath feathered over her face and it took her a moment to get her bearings once again.

To deflect, she made a little joke. "You a god of ginger, too?"

She felt him stiffen under her hands, almost like he turned into a marble statue, then he took a large step away, almost to the door of her office. She felt the loss of his body in her chest. From the doorway, he asked a soft question. "You know what I am?"

She blinked at him then waved him off. "You might be too old for it, but I know how to Google. Your name is rather unique."

He looked her up and down, as if sizing her up and finding something new and interesting. Since he was going to be all open about it, she did the same, taking in all his bronze, hard muscle on display, the twinkling onyx of his clawed feet and hands, the beautiful angles of his face. She almost lost herself in thinking about how those massive incisors of his would feel on her skin when he brought her out of her thoughts with a question. "You do not mind?"

"Mind knowing a god? It'd be awfully hypocritical of me, seeing as you keep helping me out. Plus, you are what you are. No changing that. Shitty to hold it against you."

He nodded but remained stiff, unyielding. "Unlike most humans."

"What do you mean?"

"Humans are not often so accepting, Lily."

She couldn't exactly argue with him, but there was something darker in his tone she didn't like. "Do you not like humans?" *And by extension, her*?

"I steer clear of your kind."

"Seems a bit odd," she muttered. He'd helped her multiple times and all.

"Odd is watching others like you ripped to shreds in front of your eyes by callous humans," he spit, and the force of his words, the image they brought forward, the pain she saw flash across his eyes, made her take her own step back. It was a hard jump from talk of cookies and business and ginger.

"I'm... I'm sorry." Little enough to say, but all she could muster in the moment.

"Yet another reason why I must go."

"The first reason?"

He shook his head, refusing to answer. The invisible tie binding them, making her feel him when he was near, was enough answer for her, though. If she felt it so much, as a human, surely the god felt it as well. She just needed to pull on the thread a bit, get him to acknowledge it.

She regained ground, came toward him as he loomed in her doorway. He didn't back down, didn't flinch. Appeared every bit the god, and ready to fight back, though she knew beyond a doubt he'd never harm her. Physically. "Why are you helping me so much? And why are you here?"

"I brought you what you needed." He answered only the second question, so she pressed forward, with her body and her tactics, letting her longing and feeling of rightness drive her.

"I felt you tonight."

A chill wind blasted across her front and his eyes turned more intense and probing. "How so?"

"Breeze at my back. I smelled you, too. Like a winter wind through the pines."

"You smell of ginger and flame," he admitted, then bit his lip with one sharp fang, as if he gave her too much.

Thinking she could get him to give her more, she whispered close to him, "And thanks for the book, too."

She watched the sure, stoic god snarl and back into her hallway, moving fast toward her backdoor as he kept eye contact with her. "What book?"

"The old, leather, Latin and sorta English one. Found it in my shop a few days ago. You left it, right?"

Boreas managed to somehow open the backdoor and step outside without turning from her. Lily hovered in the doorway and watched his wings flare as if he was about to take flight. "The book believes it is yours, now." That didn't exactly answer her question about the thing, but Boreas liked to only half-answer things, at least in her limited experience with the god.

Her mind blanked, though, because in that instant, he took flight. With a mighty jump into the air, his sharp, feathered wings flapped, causing a loud whoosh in the alleyway. She watched in awe as he quickly rose into the blackness of the winter night sky, losing sight of him in seconds. Lily kept her eyes trained upward despite this. Sadness and anger warred in her after he left like he did, especially because they'd had such a pleasant beginning to their little tea date. Honestly, everything about her interactions with the god left her confused. However, she remained certain about one thing: he was hers. Even if she didn't fully understand the why or the how of it all. They were bound together, ready to burn at any moment. Like wax and wick.

Chapter 5

"Ain't anybody ever told you not to do such?" Betty nagged Isa, who'd snapped closed the small pocketknife Lily'd pulled from her denim apron.

"Huh?" Isa asked Betty, eyeing her with skepticism.

"You're not supposed to go closing knives you didn't open, girl. Don't you'ns know it's bad luck?" She clucked in affront, a hen teaching a young chick what's what.

"I'm not superstitious," Isa countered, arching a brow Betty's way and ready to go toe to toe with her. This happened often, and Lily would squash it if she couldn't tell both of them secretly loved bickering with one another.

The customer, who happened to be the Baptist preacher's wife, gave a huff, at Betty and/or Isa, Lily couldn't tell, and grabbed up her bag of Christmas candles before walking out the door. Betty stared daggers at her back. Isa snorted a derisive laugh. Many in Holly Hollow respected the woman who'd stiffly walked out her door, but she always acted a bit uppity for Lily's liking, and Betty's Methodist sensibilities took umbrage at the judgement passed on her by a Baptist.

"Okay, Betty. Now, what is it you're needing?" Lily asked, trying to get everyone back on the same page. Betty had come in late in the day, after already shutting down her shop at lunchtime, to ask her some questions about the new accounting software.

"Lordy, Lily, I feel like I'm going plum crazy," she said as she reached into a huge wicker bag and pulled out an ancient laptop to plop down hard on her counter.

"Yeesh, how old is that thing?" Isa asked.

Lily might've asked the same, but she'd stopped herself. Betty was old, proud, and set in her ways. Wasn't surprising she had a laptop that looked like it'd seen better days and sounded like a brick when it hit her counter.

"It works just fine." Betty pulled out her reading glasses and flipped open the laptop. Then they waited a good five or six minutes while the thing booted up.

"Okay, look here, Lily. See this? I know it's supposed to pull direct from my cash register system, but somehow or another, it's not actually connected to the darn thing."

"Well let's see what we got here, Betty." Lily pulled the old machine her way and marveled at the heft of it.

"Shouldn't Madison be doing this?" Isa said, a sneer on her lips.

"I don't mind," Lily assured Betty.

"Oh, no, Miss Betty! I didn't mean it like that. Ain't no thing to help you out," Isa added, tossing a blindingly white smile at the woman, who caught it and tossed back her own. "Just, you know, y'all pay her for this, right?"

"Sure enough," Betty huffed out, obviously aggravated.

"Here's your issue, Betty. Your laptop needs an update to run the software correctly." Lily mentally crossed her fingers the ancient machine would support both the update and the software. Betty and Ralph may need to get a new laptop, but she'd do what she could before they went spending money they didn't need to spend.

"Seems to me Madison should be doing all this... for both of you. She don't–." The phone rang before Isa really got going, and Lily said a little thanks to the spirits for that early Christmas gift. It didn't hurt nothing to vent about people, but she didn't like to rehash old issues and dislikes over and over again.

Isa reached beside her stool to scoop up the cordless and chirped, "Lily's Lights, this is Isa. How can I help light up your Christmas today?"

Lily chuckled. They used no standard greeting for a phone call at her shop. As long as they said her shop name when they answered, Lily was fine with whatever else. She usually didn't say much more, but Isa liked to put a little sass or silliness on it, which made her laugh.

"Hello?" Isa said, her black slash of brows turning down into her frown. A few more beats then "hello?" again.

A dark pit opened up in Lily's stomach. "Hang up, Isa." She tried to go for blasé, but there must have been a tightness to her voice because both Isa and Betty stared her down.

Isa clicked the button. "What's that about?"

"Nothing. Must've been a wrong number or misdial or something."

"Didn't sound like nothing," Betty pressed.

Lily waved away their concern. "Not a big deal. Gotten a few of those recently is all."

"How many?" Isa asked as she crossed her arms over her chest, teenage demand written all over her.

"Not many."

Betty eyed her up and down, but she let it go. Mostly. "You'd tell me and my Ralph if something weird was going on with you, right?"

"Sure would, Betty." Lily smiled wide and bright. She loved her, loved she wanted to care for her, but she and Ralph had enough on their minds without worrying about weird phone calls.

"Bet," Isa said, but her tone remained unconvinced. She also, surprisingly let it go at that. Mainly because she herself had to go. "Gotta go, gang. Off to choir practice." She hopped up from her stool, went to the back to grab her bag, then moved back to wave at them. "Toodaloo lovelies!."

"Slow down, girl. Sheesh. I need to head on out, too. Got to go check on my beans."

"Will you bring me some cornbread tomorrow?" Isa asked, batting her big black lashes at Betty. Lily kind of wanted to do the same. Betty's cornbread was famous in these parts, and if she had on beans, she had a whole big pan of cornbread waiting for them, too.

Betty gave the teen a side hug as she said, "Sure thing, sugar. It'll be waiting here for you tomorrow."

"Nice," Isa said. Both headed toward the door, and she looked over her shoulder to shout, a touch too loud, "Later, boss lady."

"I'll bring you some cornbread, too," Betty called out, waving at Lily as Isa let her exit the front door first. Lily smiled at them both as they walked down the street together, Isa slowing her usual quick pace to match Betty's much slower shuffle.

"Well, shit," Lily muttered to herself an hour and a half later when she'd finished closing up. It hadn't exactly been a sunny day, but it'd been a clear winter gray when Isa and Betty left. Now, though, it was raining buckets. Actually, sleeting buckets, if the pings against her front window glass told her anything.

She'd already taken a little longer to close, and even lingered after finishing up, because of the weather. Looked to be no break in sight, so she needed to get on with it. Just sucked because she didn't have an umbrella or in the shop. It sat uselessly in the back seat of her car.

Lily internally cursed herself, but bundled up as best she could. Her puffy coat and wool cap would help, but she was going to get drenched. She cracked open the backdoor and stepped out in a rush.

She twirled around quick as a rabbit to lock the door before she noticed not a drop of anything had hit her yet. Then she caught his scent.

She turned to find Boreas standing on the edge of her parking space looking grumpy but not cold. Or wet. Both she, him, and her car appeared dry as a bone.

"What are you doing?" She meant with the magic, but really she could ask the question about anything the god did because none of it made a lick of sense to her. She wanted him with a force she'd never experienced, but damned if he didn't drive her up the wall with his hot and cold nature.

"It is sleeting," he said on a grumble.

"Okay, Captain Obvious," Lily said as she moved to her car.

His shoulders tensed at the sarcasm, and it made Lily feel bad. "Sorry. Thank you for the help. Once again." When she reached her car, she didn't get in. Instead, she turned to him and leaned her hip against her door. "Let's have another chat."

He stepped closer, frustration stretching his face tight, until he loomed only a foot away from her. His scent hit her even harder, right in the gut, and the sight of his glistening bronze skin, bunched muscles, and sharp-clawed fingers and toes made the weird pull she felt toward him thrum hard in her stomach. She became a bass string hitting a low, reverberating note.

"Lily, it is cold. The roads are getting more hazardous. You should be on your way home."

"Nope. I feel like chatting." She needed to know more. Know him. Sit with him. Above all else, she needed to do something to appease the pull she felt toward the god who continually helped her but kept apart from her.

He growled and she chuckled at the sound. After a minute-long stare down, he finally huffed and said, "At least get in the car, please." Boreas moved to her passenger seat, which was the only reason she opened the driver's side and slid inside.

"Start your vehicle."

"Yikes, bossy," she muttered.

Boreas closed his eyes, took a deep visible breath, then turned those ice blue eyes on her. "Apologies, Lily. I am merely concerned for you."

"Very concerned, given all you're doing for me lately. What you're not really doing is talking with me much. What's up with that?"

"I only wish to assist you in whatever you might need."

"Yeah. With my business, with weather protection, too, apparently, but nothing else?"

"What else do you require?" He looked hopeful, as if all he wanted in this life was to do things for her.

"I'd like to talk with you a spell. Spend time with you. Get to know you."

"Unnecessary."

"I don't think so. I think it's very necessary. Unless you want to keep acting like a creeper."

"Creeper?"

His one word, growly answers were getting annoying, and she was too tired for this mess. "Yeah. A dude who sneaks around doing secret things but doesn't engage. A creeper."

His head turned her way, and she had a flash of a hawk in the quickness and inhuman quality of the movement. "You believe I am such a creeper?"

She didn't, not really, but only because her body told her he was safe, for her at least. "No. Not really. But I don't know why. Because you're kinda acting like one, Boreas." She rested her hand on his large forearm draped on her middle console, and felt the zap of him on her skin. She shivered in response and watched his pupils dilate, blowing wide open at the simple touch. She wasn't the only one that felt whatever invisible rope stretched between them.

"Why do you always run away?" This was the million-dollar question. Lily'd never chased a man, didn't want to start now, but Boreas felt so very different, and her need for him overrode most other things. To a point. She still focused on her business. Still kept her self-respect. She, however, couldn't get him off her mind or out of her system, especially when he didn't truly explain anything or offer her relief from the ache she knew they both suffered. If only he stayed, talked, they could have more.

"I do not run," he said, hard and firm.

"You sure as hell don't stick around after you do something for me."

He sat, rigid and silent, for several long beats before he spoke again. "Do you still have the leather book?"

An odd change of subject, but Lily nodded yes. It sat on her workbench only a few feet away from where they talked.

He did give her more then. "It is a spell book. One for gods like me. I think I may have forced you to find me. With the book."

"What?"

"There are spells, magic, things you do not understand about the book and what we are to one another. However, it all comes down to one simple fact: none of this is your choice."

He looked downright miserable at the idea, but it still didn't make any sense to her. "Boreas, I have no idea what you're talking about. Something in me calls to you, I know that without doubt. Something I can't name but I know it's burrowed far down, a basic part of who I am, like my laugh or my brown hair.

I don't know anything about this magic business, but I know myself that much. No one, no thing, is making me want to be with you."

"Yes it is," he gritted out, either anger or shame flaring red across his cheeks. "It is unfair to you."

"Don't you think that's for me to decide? If you're so damn worried about me having a say in things, then maybe you should listen to what I want and, you know, give me an actual say in things."

He blinked at her then and she thought she had him, until he shook his head no. "You do not understand."

"Then make me understand," she said, reaching for his hand this time, gripping it tight and leaning across the console to get close to his face. "What I know right now is I feel right when you're around. I feel you in my gut, in my brain. That can't be a bad thing to explore, right?"

He sat a hair's breadth away, and his eyes faded from ice blue to a soft, glowing white. Fascinated, she tilted her head, leaned in closer, and breathed out, "Beautiful." By god, he was right there, so close she felt the hint of his lips on her own. Their breath mingled in the same way she wanted their limbs tangled. She almost surged up to close the last centimeter between them and taste those full lips, lick those delicious fangs of his, but before she could blink, he exited her car.

Literally, he jumped out of the car. He'd somehow gotten out of her door without her even registering the movement. He did, however, lean down to look back at her with more distance between them. She marked the missing glow and sadness in his eyes. "Goodbye, Lily."

"Goddamnit!" she yelled out as she smacked her steering wheel. The god was long gone, having jetted up into the sky as soon as he'd uttered those two parting words. She didn't know if she'd see him again. Might even bet on him being too skittish to come back. Yet the thread connecting them still hummed tight in her gut. If he felt the same, she wanted to believe he'd come back despite his reservations. Yet, she'd learned long ago that words, actions, and feelings were like mixing new candle scents. Just because she thought it should all work didn't mean it came out lovely in the end.

Chapter 6

Lily opened her shop as usual on Monday, running through her to-do list as she hung her coat and purse in the storage room and made her way to the front. She usually arrived at 8AM, an hour before the shop opened, to get anything she needed in order and ease her way into her day. This day, however, the shrill ring of a phone jostled her easy morning routine. She reached for the cordless as she looked over the latest orders she'd received from her Etsy shop. The thought that she might just need to get her own web shop running, a big financial leap she'd probably, disappointingly, need to talk to Madison about, flitted through her head as she absently answered the phone. "Lily's Lights. How can I help you?"

Nothing. She waited a long ten seconds before again speaking. "Hello?"

Again, nothing. Just like the weird calls at her house and shop and the one call Isa took. She'd figured they were prank calls from some kid in the area. Still, it made the spot between her shoulders ache with tension the longer it went on.

Instead of talking to nothing, she hung up, suppressing the not-fun shiver down her spine as she stared at the phone. She'd had weird calls before, long looks from a distance, for a time in her life, but the calls then had involved screaming or crying or pleading. Never silence.

She just hoped like hell the source of those calls years ago wasn't up to his old tricks. Ryan had moved back to town according to all the gossip, but she'd yet to see him. She wanted to keep it that way, though it'd be hard in a tiny place like Holly Hollow.

Sadly, her worries were confirmed around lunchtime that day. She spent her lunch as usual, eating her turkey sandwich at her counter and catching up on web things as she did, when the tinkle of the bell at her door made her look up. The bright customer-service smile she aimed at the door wilted quickly when she saw the man striding through it.

Ryan stood there, his navy wool suit and matching overcoat immaculate, a red tie bright against the lighter blue undershirt over his chest. If she could achieve a detached perspective, she might be able to say he was handsome in an all-American football player way: dirty blond hair trimmed short, no trace of facial hair, interesting hazel eyes, tall frame, wide chest, muscled limbs she could tell he maintained despite the time between last seeing him. Still, he lacked the icy gaze and gravitas of a certain god she'd recently met. He'd also broken her heart because he was a dirty rotten cheater, so she wasn't too keen on admitting anything good about the man.

"Lily," he said, his voice firm and saccharine, sickly sweet to her ears.

"Hello, Ryan," she replied, staring. Waiting. Knowing he would do something that'd piss her off shortly.

He stood in the center of her shop, hands stuffed into the pockets of his trousers, surveying the place. Evaluating it like he wanted to invest in her business. It ruffled her feathers for sure, but she waited for more.

"Your place looks good, Lil. I like it." He smiled wide her way, and Lily stiffened at the pet name no one had called her in a good seven years and continued to just stare at the man.

He chuckled, as if finding her lack of enthusiasm adorable, and wandered over to a display of the ginger cookie candles. One of his fingers stroked down a jar and it made Lily sneer, not liking him being near any part of something she'd made.

To be honest, Lily hadn't thought about Ryan in a long time. At least before he moved back to town. She'd moved on. Felt indifferent at best. Despite that, the man coming into her space made her feel off. Her shop, her business—it had been something he'd never touched because she started it up after they were done. Now he had. He'd stepped right into her current life and she didn't want him wrecking it like he had her past.

"Can I help you find something, Ryan?" Best to get the interaction over with and move on.

He shrugged, then grabbed a jar, examining the candle he rolled in his hands. Ryan tossed it gently up, but it caught enough air Lily worried it'd shatter on the floor. He managed to catch it with a grin her way and moved slowly toward her counter. "I think I'll take this. My mama said she saw one at Sandy Owen's place and loved the smell."

Ryan's mom had always acted polite but distant, and had never stepped foot in her store despite being around the small town all the time. Lily had never minded, never blamed her for being loyal to her son. Guess she liked her products, though.

Lily nodded and bent down to get a bag and a sheet of tissue paper. When she came up, there he stood, looming far too close. Not in the delicious way Boreas loomed, and for a second, she lingered on the stark difference between these two.

Pulled back from her thoughts of the god by Ryan inching closer, she said, "Back up, Ryan." Her hand pushed the air between them, like she could shove him over with a wind she couldn't control.

He put his hands up in front of him with a good-old-boy posture that caused Lily's anger to rise quickly. "No harm intended," he said and made a show of looking away, surveying her shop once more. "Business good?" he asked, but Lily didn't answer. She rung up the sale, wrapped the candle and cradled it in the bag.

"That'll be 15.89," she finally said, nodding toward the small credit card box at the edge of the counter. Ryan made a big show of pulling out a shiny black credit card and tapping it to pay. She ripped off the receipt as soon as it spit out of the machine.

"There you go," she said, handing it over to him and encouraging Ryan to move on with everything she had.

He cocked his head at her. "Really, Lily? You still gonna act like this?"

"Like what?"

"Like you don't care."

With a heavy sigh, she crossed her arms at her chest. "Surprisingly, Ryan, I actually don't care. Not anymore. Not for a long time."

"I think you just might," he whispered, leaning in close and winking in her face. A wink that would have made her melt seven years ago made her sneer now.

"What exactly do you want here, Ryan?"

He straightened, turned serious, and said, "I thought we could go out. Catch up. Tonight, when you close up."

"I'm open late tonight." Like every other shop in downtown Holly Hollow, she stayed open late the second Monday of every month, for people who needed more shopping time and the occasional vampire who came through the town.

"I know, darling," he drawled. "After."

"No."

"That's it. Just 'no?'"

"It's a complete sentence."

His face changed and she recognized the swift shift. Ryan never liked it when he didn't get his way. Just so happened she didn't care. She also didn't have to put up with it anymore, and if she was honest with herself, shouldn't have put up with it for so long in her past. "We're done here, Ryan."

"Oh, I don't think so, sweet Lily," he whispered, a trace of menace there.

Done with this, done with him, she switched tactics. "You been calling me?" Years ago, he'd harassed her until her brother put an end to it with threats. Ryan was the type of dude who respected men's threats, especially men who could beat his ass.

Now, however, her brother lived too far to threaten anyone here, and Ryan would see that as an opportunity.

He smiled at her, neither confirming nor denying.

"Stop it," she said, stretching herself taller, ready to stand her ground.

"You look good, Lil," he said out of nowhere, his blue eyes sweeping down then up her body. She sneered at the audacity and decided he needed to go. Right this minute.

Lucky for her, she didn't have to push him out on her own. In that instant, the bell sounded, and Betty stalked through the door with Ralph at her back, both huffing with anger.

"Whatcha doing in here, Ryan Moore?" Betty bit out, stopping only a foot from him to glare. Ralph loomed at her back, an old but solid presence.

"Just buying a Christmas gift," he said, snatching up his bag.

"Humph. Looks like it's bought. Now you should get."

Ryan laughed. "Okay Mrs. Booth." He headed for the door then looked back at Lily from over his shoulder. "See you around, Lil."

Ralph squinted at the man who chuckled and strolled out as if he had not a care in the world.

Betty fumed. "Saw that snake when I brought in the sandwich board for the day. Grabbed my Ralph."

"Thanks, Betty." Lily doubted they intimidated Ryan, but he hated making a scene in front of others, so their presence did help. "Appreciate it."

"Ppssshhh. Next time he comes in, just bang on the wall and we'll come running. Ralph is hell with a rolling pin."

Lily laughed at the visual: seventy-five-year-old Ralph slowly chasing Ryan around the shop with a heavy wooden rolling pin. Her laughter cleared when she thought she might need help. Ryan never gave up easily. His calls would probably escalate, too, now that he knew she knew who made them. "Will do," she answered, a bit more serious. Maybe a bit more worried. And just when everything looked all merry and bright, too.

———

At ten to nine, ten minutes before she closed the shop, the vampire who'd perused the candles on display for the last ten minutes let out a low, dangerous hiss. Lily, frightened, whipped her head toward the lithe woman. Her ghostly pale face, framed by ringlets of auburn hair, zeroed in not on Lily, but the back of the shop. Without a word or looking away from the spot where she stared, the woman set down the candle she'd been holding and slowly backed out of the store. Her eyes didn't break their stare until she turned to run away, too fast for Lily to track.

Heart beating hard in her chest, Lily gripped the counter and let out a harsh breath. She was thankful Isa had left an hour earlier. Nothing had happened, and there were few accounts of humans being attacked by vampires for no good reason, but they were still predators. Lily'd never felt that more than just then.

Given what happened, Lily moved to her front door, flipped the open sign to closed, and locked the door. There weren't many still wandering the streets now, so closing a few minutes early seemed just fine by her. She quickly did her closing routine, flipped off all her lights except the small lamp she kept going in the lab, and bundled up in her thick coat.

She hesitated at the door, her heart once again racing. Lily didn't know what had spooked the vampire, but something had. What if something scarier than a vampire waited out there? Shaking her head to loosen up the fear, she decided to push ahead. There were still plenty of people about, what with all the shops closing. A loud enough scream would hopefully bring some people running if she needed them.

As she pushed the door open, a little more cautiously than normal, a sharp sound cracked. She jumped about a mile but steadied herself quickly when nothing came rushing at her. Her head poked out first, looking around at the dark alleyway. She didn't see anything. Until she looked down at the back stoop.

A large stick leaned against the back wall, honed wood gleaming in the yellowish light of the covered bulb hovering above her backdoor. It looked massive, yes, but it was just a stick. Her hand shot down to grab it as she stepped fully from the door, letting it close firmly behind her.

It was a walking stick. Hand-carved, its intricate design popped out at her in the darkness. The deep grooves and swirls and swoops moved through images of tree-lined mountains. After she turned it over in her hand a minute or two, she realized what it represented: wind in the pines. Exactly as she'd described Boreas's scent to him.

Her breath caught, hope welled, and she called out "Boreas?" No one answered. She knew he wouldn't. His scent didn't hit her nose and the tightrope between them sat unmoving in her chest, no signal of him being close at hand.

Disappointment stung, but made a new resolve form in her mind. She yearned, a feeling she'd never experienced before, but she also thought. Thought about Ryan—what he'd done that day and in the past—and how regardless of need or want or desire, she would remain in control. She was no delicate snowflake blown about in a storm.

Chapter 7

"Sorry I can't make it home for Christmas, sis."

Lily leaned her head against her cell, trapping it between her ear and shoulder so she had her hands free to finish up her dinner. "I'd sure like to see you, bub, but I understand you can't get off the rig. No harm, except you'll miss Betty's Christmas cookies."

"Ugh, don't go reminding me. Food is shit here and I don't want to think on what I'm missing."

Lily laughed at her brother then tapped her wooden spoon against the lip of the saucepan, letting the plain marinara she'd thrown on the stove from a jar when she'd gotten home simmer. She'd drained the pasta in the sink already, and Betty had given her half a loaf of braided rosemary garlic bread, so she was good to go. Nothing fancy, but she rarely went fancy when she ate alone, which was most nights.

"Oh, do be on the lookout. I sent you presents. Might even be some things in there from Miss Betty."

"That's what I like to here, sis," he said. "Otherwise, what's going on with you? How you been?"

Lily couldn't rightly answer. Not that she didn't know the truth: things were hectic and stressful on many different levels.

She didn't want to lay that at her brother's feet and make him feel even worse about not being home for the holidays. Instead, she put fake cheer in her voice when she said "Same old, same old, brother. Nothing ever new happens around these parts, which is how I like it."

"The shop doing well?"

"Yep," she popped out as she pulled down a plate and scooped up cutlery from her silverware drawer. This at least wasn't a lie. She sold out her candles as quick as she could make them these days, or just about. She'd need to hustle the next few days to make sure she had enough for the Christmas Masquerade.

The Holly Hollow Christmas Masquerade was legend. It'd been going on for a few decades now, well before they revamped downtown. It used to be a rowdy time. Now, it catered to a more sophisticated crowd. Big time horse money had latched onto it some time ago, making it the in thing to do during the holiday season, and they continued to come, bringing in fancy dresses and much needed tourist dollars to her town.

Nothing for her to complain about because she made a mint during and after, but she still remembered the small community feel of the event in her youth, and then it maybe had a bit more cheer to it.

She also couldn't complain about the magic still there: beautiful dresses and elaborate masks and good food and mulled wine. All of it had its own warmth to it. She was particularly happy to wear the wool dress Isa's mama made for her. Which reminded her, she needed to finish up hot gluing beads to her half mask.

"Okey-doke, bub. I gotta get off here. Dinner's waiting."

"Right. Talk to you soon, sis. Love ya."

"Love ya too," she said before she slid the phone from the crook of her neck and caught it in a quick swooping movement. He'd already hung up, so she laid it face down on her counter, gathered her food, and made her way to the couch, where she did most of her eating.

Sitting crossed legged right in the middle of the cozy cushions, she flipped on the TV and went right to one of her supernatural comfort shows. Lily half watched as she slurped up sauced up spaghetti and dipped Betty's beautiful bread in sauce. The show entertained her, as always, but she'd seen the episode umpteen times, so it didn't keep her mind from wandering.

Lily thought on her issue with Ryan. She hated to admit it, even to herself, but he was a problem she needed to solve sooner rather than later. Hoping he'd take a hint and leave her alone wasn't working. She couldn't figure what to do, but she feared it'd get worse before it got better. Sadly, things like this often had to get worse before a woman could get the law to help her out.

A funny idea struck her: she had one man she couldn't get rid of and another she couldn't get to stick around.

Boreas, the monstrous god she wanted far more than any human man she'd ever known, wouldn't give her the time of day. She felt it between them, a connection like a chain wrapping around her gut and pulling her toward him. She didn't mind it. He seemed grumpy but solid. A good sort of man.

He, however, seemed to mind it a whole hell of a lot. Which she didn't fully get. He thought something in that old book made her gravitate toward him. What he couldn't get through his pretty but thick head was she didn't care how it happened because she was happy it had. She wanted him, enjoyed the small bits of time she'd spent with him, appreciated all he'd done for her and knew he would continue to do for her. She just wanted more. She wanted everything from him. But she'd be damned if she'd beg any man for attention.

Ripping a hunk of bread off with her teeth she muttered, "Ain't no way." She'd have all of Boreas or she'd kick him to the curb. She wouldn't live her life pining for a god who seemed determined to not be a part of it. It might hurt like hell, but the respect she'd lose for herself—the same hard-won respect she'd gained after dropping Ryan all those years ago —was more precious than half-moments with someone.

Two nights after her resolution, exhaustion wracked her body. She'd stayed late to finish up making candles for the Christmas Masquerade. She'd barely done it, but she'd done it. There were plenty of small and large tapers for the event and lots of stock to set out the night of and restock the next day.

Her hands ached from sharp splashes of wax during the long process, so she rubbed thick aloe on her skin for relief before she slipped out the back door. She shoved the key in the lock and turned it, giving a tired exhale. "What're you doing here again, Boreas?" without even turning to him. She knew he stood behind her somewhere, smelled it right away on the wind. Felt his nearness pulling at her.

He was less than a foot away when she spun around, but she held her ground. His face was pinched, and he grabbed her hands before she could protest. She hissed in pain at the contact. Boreas tutted low in his throat. "What happened?"

He hadn't answered her question, so she didn't feel like answering his. "I'm tired and just want to go home." She tried to pull her hands away, but his clawed fingers held them in their grip, though it was a gentle hold. Knowing he'd not let go unless she told him, she caved. "A hazard of the job, I'm afraid. Had to make a ton of candles, so I got burned by stray wax."

"Why do you not wear gloves?"

"Oh, thank you, ol' mighty god of wind. I'd never have thought of that without you."

He paused his study of her hands to look up into her face, worry replaced by confusion. "Why do you seem so angry?"

"I don't know, Boreas. Maybe it's because you swoop in at night, make demands of me, and then fly off without me having any say in the matter."

He stiffened, straightening his spine so he came to his full, impressive height. Lily stayed firmly in her anger and decided to ignore the tingling feeling of him looming over her with his height and bulk in the dark cold winter night. "You don't understand–"

"You *think* I don't understand, what with my delicate human woman brain and all."

"That is not what I meant, Lily."

She tried again to twist her hands free, but they really did hurt, so it was a half-hearted attempt at best. "Then what do you mean? Because from where I'm standing, you've explained your position to me, and I've told you it's bullshit."

"My reservations are not bullshit," he said, heat now tingeing his voice for the first time.

"Oh yeah they are, especially as they give me no say in my own life." He blinked in surprise and she kept right on going. "That's right, mister mighty god man. You're doing to me exactly what you say you're trying to protect me from. You say I had no choice, but I'm standing here, telling you I choose you, and you straight up ignore what I'm saying."

"But the book..."

"Gods damn the book!" she yelled in his face, going in close. "It's a stupid ass book. Might be magic or whatever, but it can't control what I think or do, no matter what you think. I control that. Maybe it brought me to you, brought us together, but nothing more."

He rocked back on his heels, like he'd been hit clear in the chest with her words. After several beats he whispered, "I am sorry."

"What?" In her experience, men rarely apologized, especially when they were wrong.

"I am sorry, Lily. All you say is true. The book... there are things you do not fully know, but it cannot manipulate any being's thoughts or actions without their consent. Feelings are a different story, or may possibly be. The intricacy of emotions versus thoughts are complex. Nevertheless, I should have listened to you, rather than staying frozen in my own understanding of the situation. For this, I am sorry."

"Well... okay then." Lily deflated, her anger flowing out of her body in a quick stream. Boreas gave her a tentative smile, one fang flashing in the light over her back door, and she melted more.

"May I help?" he asked, lifting her hands slightly to indicate what he meant.

"If you can, have at it."

Boreas turned her hands over in his giant mitts, studying the splotchy red marks. In all honesty, her hands were mostly immune to it at this point, like a chef being toughened by basic burns, but when she made too many candles or worked for too long, she'd end up with at least a few sensitive spots.

Boreas hefted a breath, and she felt the wind rush into him, as if going home, before he bent low to blow across her hands. A chilly wind wrapped around her, cooling the burns better than the aloe cream ever could. She sighed in relief, and he straightened, a happy light dancing in his ice blue eyes.

"Thank you. Feels mighty good." The wind continued to wrap around her hands, gently relieving all the ache there. Boreas nodded in acknowledgement and took a step back from her.

"So..." She was unsure where they stood now. He'd helped her once again, which he always did, but he'd also apologized for his previous behavior. She wondered if it meant he wanted to see more of her. The first excuse she grasped onto to spend time together popped up pretty damn quick. "There's this big Christmas party in the middle of town this coming Wednesday. Would you like to come with me?"

"I do not know if I can do that, Lily."

"But–"

He stopped her with a hand in the air. "You were correct in your assessment of the situation, and I am going to make myself more accustomed to the idea of you having choice in the matters between us." All good to hear, but he kept on going. "However, I am as I am. What I am is typically not accepted by groups of humans, even if a single human can do so."

Lily considered it. He'd always met her in private, in the dark. Made sense if he worried about what others might see and think, even do, especially given the bloody history he'd hinted at before. He wasn't exactly wrong, either. People were often good, kind, accepting. Groups of people on the other hand––they could be volatile and unpredictable. All of history'd proven that more than a time or two.

"If we become something, is this how it will always be between us? Stolen moments in the dark?" It made her sad to consider such a life.

He stepped back into her, hugging her to him so his warmth soaked in deep in a few long beats. "My kind has a long and sordid relationship with humanity, Lily. You must understand this if we are to continue together."

"I get it, I do, but it seems harder than it has to be." Lily also didn't want to think badly of her neighbors, most of whom she'd known her whole life. She'd hope they'd see who he was, and who he was to her, and accept him. Then again, the Christmas Masquerade filled up with lots of people, not just her neighbors in Holly Hollow.

"I am uncertain how I may proceed because I have always kept myself apart from humans. I can investigate, but I cannot give you a promise."

"Even if I ask nicely?" She fluttered her lashes at him in an exaggerated way, hoping some humor might alleviate the stress etched in the lines of his usually smooth face.

He did crack a fanged smile, which turned hungry in an instant, and the heat of the moment blossomed despite the cold wind he still twirled around her hands. "My Lily," he whispered. "How you surprise me."

She wanted to give him surprises every day for the rest of his life, and the idea startled her. Mainly because as soon as she thought it she knew it to be true. Instead of dwelling, she gave him another surprise. She went up on her tippy toes and gave him a quick peck on the lips.

Well, she'd intended it to be a quick peck, but as soon as her lips met his, he gripped her in a tight hug and dragged her up his body, taking her mouth in a searing, demanding kiss. This was no sweet peck. Heat, want, and need welled up between them. She forgot about her sore hands and gripped the back of his head, digging her fingers into the silky white strands of his hair.

He growled down her throat, bending her back as he stroked his tongue across her own. She gasped at the contact then felt bereft. Suddenly he stood a few feet away, much like he'd done when they'd almost kissed in her car. Except she knew his taste now, and she didn't want to let him go.

"Boreas," she moaned, all the lust coursing through her veins making her voice husky.

CHILLY LITTLE THING

He bit out a curse in some other language and panted, but did not return to her. "No, Lily. I must see if I can be a part of the life you wish to lead."

"Do what now?" She wasn't stupid, but the kiss had made her a little lust drunk, so she had a hard time following.

Boreas stepped closer, reaching out a hard to trace a sharp claw down her cheek. "Your beautiful flush is something I wish to see again," he whispered. "However, I must first discover if I can give you what you ask of me."

"The Christmas Masquerade isn't all that important," she admitted.

"No, Lily. It is more than a singular event. If we are to truly be together, such questions will continue to arise between us. I must know if I can be what you need. You must be assured I can be in your life in all ways. You, my Lily, deserve more than half-measures."

"But you don't know if you can?"

His shoulders fell when he answered, "No. I do not know for certain."

A crack snaked right down her heart, but she understood. He didn't want to start something he couldn't finish. Sucked, but might also be the best way for them to move forward. "I hope I see you at the masquerade. I hope-- I hope I see you again." She had to say it, because in the moment it felt like if he could not find an acceptable answer she might not ever see him again. The possibility of such a thing, the uncertainty, made her even more heartsick.

"So do I, my Lily."

Wind kissed her lips and the god shot into the air, off to find whatever answers he needed to give her what she wanted.

Chapter 8

Lily fussed over the candles on display, pushing her half-mask up into her slicked back brown hair, causing a small tuft to stick out at an odd angle.

"For crying out loud," she muttered as she shoved the wisps away, starting her count again.

"We're good, Lily," Isa said. The teen swayed gently in her black and gold silk dress. Her mama, Maria, made the gorgeous thing. She made all of Isa's dresses for such occasions. The silk flowed like water, spilling over the girl, gathering at one side in a small circlet on her waist, the intermixed strips of gold and black dripping down to the floor. It was a thing of beauty, but for not the first time Lily wondered how she wasn't cold. There were sleeves, but silk wasn't exactly the warmest of fabrics. She chalked it up to the universal truth that teens never seemed to get cold and didn't think too much more on it.

Isa's mama made Lily's Christmas Masquerade dress, too. Much different in design, but no less gorgeous. It was deep maroon wool, tight from the neck down, along her sleeves, and to her waist where it flared in a shape that reminded her of the top of a heart. From there, pleated maroon wool created a voluminous skirt that flitted about her legs whenever she moved.

She'd taken a swatch of the same fabric and covered her eye mask with it, dotting clusters of gold and pearl beads at the corners of the eyes for a simple but elegant look. However, it currently sat on her head so it was out of her way, making her hair all wonky.

"I'm just checking," Lily muttered as Isa ignored her worrying and hummed along to the bluegrass quartet playing on the small makeshift stage in the middle of the street. She not only checked. She also fretted. Candles were something she could fuss over, unlike her increasing worry about the fate of her and a certain god.

"You wanna go dance?" Lily asked after noticing Isa's sway. The town used her candles to light the night at the Christmas Masquerade, just like they used the Booth's cookies and the coffee shop's roast for the snack table. It started as a purely local event, and even as it expanded for tourists to come in, they liked to keep the products local. They also allowed the shops to put out small displays of goods for sale. A good chance for the money from around Lexington to buy while they danced.

"Nah. Ain't no one here to dance with," Isa said before she took a seat at her stool behind the table. Lily looked over the crowd, catching several teen boys stealing glances at Isa, but said nothing. Wasn't her place to pry.

"Fair enough," Lily said before a woman in a white gown and rabbit-fur hat strolled up and distracted her.

As she put the woman's purchase in her bag and thanked her, Lily heard Isa say, "Maybe I was wrong," in a breathy whisper.

Lily glanced up and froze, a chilly wind pushing through the wall of her skirts as she locked eyes with Boreas, who stood about ten feet away, staring back.

CHILLY LITTLE THING

Isa noticed the stare, too, and Lily's freeze. Immediately sitting up straight, she asked "Who *is* that, Lily?"

The candlemaker couldn't answer her. She was transfixed by the way the god glided toward her, his legs strong and his gait steady, but somehow still looking as if helped along by a self-created wind at his heels. She'd never seen him in anything other than the toga. Made sense to her, he was an old Greek god after all. Just then, however, he wore a navy suit, shirt, and tie all the same color of winter sky. It molded to his body, highlighting his delicious muscles with every movement. A small navy eye mask with golden stars scattered across it sparkled on his face and made his brilliant blue eyes pop. His bronze skin nearly glowed in the candlelight and his snow-white hair glinted and twinkled like spun silver, even pulled back in a thick ponytail as it was.

After taking in all the deliciousness, something hit her a second too late. His hands. No claws. She flipped her gaze down to see his feet, claws usually on full display, clad in shiny dark brown dress shoes. Her gaze moved to his mouth; the shape smoothed as if his fangs were gone. A frown creased her brow as he stepped fully up to the table.

"Lily," he said, his growl firmly in place yet somehow questioning in tone.

"Boreas," she said with a nod, not able to get out much more with the relief she felt at the sight of him.

A loud clearing of a throat sounded at her side and she jumped in surprise. "Oh, yeah. Isa, this is Boreas. Boreas, this is Isa."

"A pleasure," the god said, giving the teen a bow and smile but turning his attention back to Lily without a second glance.

"Same," Isa said, and despite not looking at her, Lily could hear the sly smile in her voice.

"Music's good, ain't it?" Isa asked. Boreas gave another nod her way. Lily felt Isa's elbow clip her side and she turned to look at the girl, breaking her gaze with the god with reluctance. Isa didn't say anything, but she didn't need to. She wasn't being subtle. Instead, she waggled her perfectly manicured eyebrows at Lily and flicked her head at the god in the universal symbol of "Go on, then."

Before Lily could, Boreas spoke. "Lily, it would please me a great deal if you would give me your hand." He looked oddly flushed. "For this next dance."

Isa giggled a teen girl giggle and Lily hesitated. She looked to her table, but before she could deny him, despite what she wished, Isa piped up. "I have this, Lily." She looked to her phone and said, "We should be packing up anyway."

"If we're packing up..."

"I got this," Isa repeated slowly for emphasis, practically shoving Lily around the side of the table to stand beside Boreas. He looked her up and down, a shiver of wind trailing where his icy eyes landed. His nostrils flared and he closed those eyes, visibly taking in a long, deep breath. Holding out his hand to her, he waited. She frowned down at it once again but placed her human hand in his usually not-so-human one.

They walked to the small dance floor, people staring as they did. Lily wasn't one to date around, but it wasn't odd to see her out on the occasional date. This was different, and everyone sensed it. Madison, clad in a shimmery, slinky dress, stared openly, slack jawed. Ryan, who'd been chatting in a group of his old high school friends, the big man back in town, had kept his distance but watched her all evening. Now, his face went red and his eyes went hard before he slammed down the mulled wine in his hand and stalked off somewhere beyond the warm glow of lights and candles surrounding the Christmas festivities.

Lily didn't mind any of it. She focused on Boreas. The heat of his hand, the feel of his skin on hers. The tingle down her spine when he gently spun her so she landed in his outstretched arms, fitting just right against his chest as they began to dance.

Absurdly, the first thing she blurted out was "You know how to two-step?"

Boreas smiled down at her, his mask moving up slightly at the rise of his cheeks. "Yes, Lily. I know many dances. It's one of the things I love about..."

He trailed off so Lily didn't know if he meant humans or life in general, but the idea brought her back to another question. "What's up with your hands?"

Said hand flexed in her own, gripping her tight. "The thing I went off to find allows me to mask my form. I knew such trinkets once existed, but did not know if they still did, or if I could acquire one."

"Why didn't you just tell me that instead of leaving me worrying over you?" Lily felt happy to see him, but also annoyed that all he needed was some simple thing he went to fetch.

"I am sorry I did not clarify, but there was more. I needed to discuss effectiveness and life as a god in human form with someone who knew more than me. How long, how well, it might work for one such as me." His words were hushed so no one else could hear, meaning he whispered them with hot breath across her cold ear, warming her in many ways.

Lily wasn't exactly appeased, but they could work on better communication. Now, having him with her in public, holding her tight, whispering in her ear seemed enough. Still, a few more answers wouldn't hurt. "Another–" she almost said god but stopped herself as another couple twirled close. "A relative?"

He smiled at her coded language. "Of a sort. Someone I have known all my life but one who spent a great deal of time amongst people such as you."

"Not all of you hide away?"

He laughed. "No, and this particular someone lives a very ostentatious life, when they are out in the world. They do tend to flit in and out on a whim."

Lilylingered on the feel of his non-clawed hand. She thought it off, unnatural. "How does this work?" she asked on a squeeze of the hand.

"A magic amulet renders me like this as long as I wear it," he explained before he slowed a step. "Do you prefer it?"

She shook her head violently. "No. I find this... odd. I like the real you."

He didn't reply, but a small smile stretched across his face. Lily stared at it, the way it transformed his grumpy demeanor and caused a twinge of something in her chest.

"Thank you," she whispered. He nodded, again not replying but acknowledging what he'd done for her.

The twang of the fiddle faded all too soon, and on the last note, Boreas dipped her low. His face came in close, so close she thought he'd kiss her. Instead, he put his warm nose against her cold cheek, smelled deep, and ran it down the line of her jaw. "Sweet, sweet Lily," he muttered before he brought her back upright.

Her heart stomped out its own rapid dance in her chest, but she pushed through to whisper. "Uh, would you like some mulled wine? Coffee? Cookies?"

At the word "cookies," Betty suddenly appeared at her side, shoving one of her Christmas treats right in Boreas face. "I'm Mrs. Betty Booth. Seems you know my girl Lily, so it's nice to meet you, young man."

Lily giggled like Isa at the young man comment, amused by her friend and giddy on dancing with the god. Of course, Boreas, despite the white hair, looked younger than Betty. Still, he had millennia on her.

He blinked down at the stooped older woman then gave a firm, knowing nod. The serious look on his face transferred to the cookie she'd somehow slipped in his hand without either of them noticing. "Thank you," he said after a few beats. "A pleasure to meet you as well, ma'am."

Betty beamed at his words and gave an ogling look between Lily and Boreas. She didn't know the god, obviously, but she caught something about him she liked, giving Lily her own waggling eyebrow version of "Go on, then."

"I'll leave you young'uns to it," she said with a clap of her hands. "Nights are for lovers and such. Not for old women with weary bones. Me and mine are off for the evening." Betty gestured toward Ralph, who already had their table cleared and looked more than ready to go. Lily looked to her own spot, seeing it cleared away. "That Isa is a good girl, she is. Already has your stuff carted back to the store. Nothing more for you to do here."

Lily was about to say she should check on everything when Betty said, "It's all taken care of, dear. Now get." She literally shooed them off, like stray cats asking for extra dinner after she gave out her scraps.

Lily huffed out a laugh and felt Boreas take her hand once again. "May I walk you to your car?" She smiled, bright as the stars, and said, "Sure." The word may have been a little breathy, but no one would blame her when she had a god holding her hand and being so chivalrous.

She'd parked behind her store, so they only had a few blocks to stroll. When they were out of earshot of most people, she asked, "I assume, since you are here, you found the answers you needed to be with me, here and now."

He paused, her arms snagging, as she'd kept on moving, so she had to step back and face him.

"Yes. Plutus helped, but more so you. You were right, Lily. If I'm being true to myself and what we have, I should not question it. I should be here, fully and completely, in the life you have in this town. Now, I know for certain I can." His voice was light on the wind but hard in tone as he cupped her head in his massive hand. She wished his claws were on her cheek in that moment.

"I don't want you changing for me," she countered. "That wasn't what I meant at all." She wanted him, yes, but not at his expense.

"No, Lily. I have not changed. Not exactly. I... just have a new perspective. A new purpose. You give me reason to be of this world instead of apart from it."

"I don't care much about purpose right now. Only that you're here, with me, showing you want to be here. With me." Lily whispered as she moved closer, leaning into his broad, warm chest as she reached up to cling to his shoulders.

"Lily, you and I... there's more to this than you know."

"I don't give a shit, Boreas. All I care about right now is you kissing me."

A rumble ripped up his chest, so strong she felt it where she leaned against him. His head dipped low, and the sweet scent of pine filled her nose as a quick breeze whipped around them, raising her hair as it did. Boreas paused, groaned as if he lost something, then took her lips with his own.

It was an owning, a claiming, that much Lily knew. Down to her toes. An arc of energy rippled through her in a line straight from her lips to her core, causing her to melt into him even more. He moved his lips expertly, with lethal precision. Nibbling, licking, he worked his lips over hers, warming her heart and body in equal measure. When he gave a particularly quick nip, Lily gasped at the sensation, opening up more for him. Boreas took full advantage, his tongue moving in to caress her own.

He pressed into her and pulled her to him at the same time, bending her back as he'd done in their dance. Lily clung to him, wanting more. Wanting whatever he would give her. Thinking only of want, actually, as he kissed her silly.

His mouth moved away from her own and she groaned in disappointment. The groan turned to a moan, however, when his lips and tongue didn't move away but instead moved down, trailing fire from her lips to her cheek to her neck.

"You taste exquisite, my Lily," he muttered, his words slightly slurred as if he were drunk. Lily thought he might be a bit tipsy on lust if he felt anything like she did.

She gave a hiss when she felt a sharp tooth snag against the skin of her neck, wanting more, unable to contain the surge of desire it brought out in her.

Boreas, however, righted them both, and stepped a good five feet away from her.

"What? Why?"

"Did I hurt you?" Pain sliced across his face, and Lily ached for him.

"Oh, honey. No. Not at all. It felt good. So, so good."

She didn't wait for him to come back to her. Instead, she moved as swiftly as her human feet allowed, practically jumping back into his arms. He caught her with ease, bringing her body up his own so she stared down into his face. She bent, kissed him again, and felt warm in the cold winter night.

He eased her back down, moving them step by step until they were in the darker shadows of an alley. Only then did his hands roam in slow slides up and down her sides, teasing the edges of her hips and breasts. Boreas paused high up her bodice, his hands hovering in silent question at her breasts. "Yes," she moaned out as she peppered his face with kisses.

Those strong, sure hands skimmed her breasts over her dress, but it still felt like a hot iron blazing across her chest. She bucked at the sensation, bringing her hips tight in line with his, then moaning at the hard length pressing back against her.

He cursed in some language she didn't know and moved his mouth to her ear, sucking as his hands moved to her ass, forced it up, so she instinctively wrapped her legs around him. Not an easy task in a winter dress, but the voluminous skirt gave her a little more wiggle room than most. And thank all the gods out there, because when he pinned her to the ice-cold brick of the alley wall with his hips, grinding into her already soaking core, she nearly let out a scream of ecstasy.

Lily'd never felt this riled, this turned on, in her entire life. She was no virgin or prude, but something in the twang of feeling between her and Boreas made the lust ride strong and hard through her veins. It heightened everything. So much so she might orgasm in the cold night from him simply grinding against her for a few minutes. She didn't care one bit about where they kissed or how quickly it all had come on. She only cared about feeling him, tasting him, getting as close to the god as she physically could.

Sadly, for her, he stopped abruptly. He dropped her hips so she had to uncurl her legs from his waist and right herself.

She gave out a clear huff of protest, but something had snagged his attention to their left. He growled in a not-so-sexy way, and, with a quick side-step, put her at his back as he faced the darker recesses of the alley. She peeked around his big-even-in-human form and looked for clues in the small, dark space.

After several tense beats, Ryan strolled out, hands in his pockets, as if he had not a care in the world. "You okay, Lil?" His voice dripped with fake worry, but a hard glint of anger shone clear in his eyes.

"Damnit, Ryan. Why are you skulking about in the dark?"

"Just making sure you're okay, Lil," he said again, not sparing a look her way. Instead, he stared at Boreas. His ego made him do it, but the barely leashed power and violence under the surface of the god meant the stare down didn't last long. Ryan lost, looking away first. Boreas never took his hawkish eyes off him, even after he looked away.

"I'm fine. More importantly, it's none of your damn business, Ryan. I told you before: leave me alone."

Boreas growled again at her words. Ryan did his good-old-boy head shake. "I'm keeping an eye out is all. You need anything, anything at all, you know where to find me."

The man strolled away, and Lily had to give it to him. To be able to look so nonchalant when a god breathed down your neck was a feat. Except Ryan knew nothing about Boreas's godhood. He might whistle a different tune if he knew.

"I'm so sorry about that," she said, ready to explain Ryan, but Boreas once again surprised her.

"He's following you. Harassing you. And you don't like it."

"How do you know?"

"His scent, and the way yours changed when he appeared."

Not much she could hide from him with that godly nose. "He's an ex. Newly back in town. He wants another chance and I don't want to give it to him."

"He's more dangerous than he looks," Boreas said.

"Aren't most men?"

He stared at her a moment, sad understanding flashing on his face, and he nodded. Taking her hand, Boreas brought it up to his lips and kissed the back. "Come, sweet Lily. Let's get you home."

Ryan had messed with the mood, for sure, but it still saddened her that the god didn't want to pick back up with their make out session. Like a damned perfect gentleman, he walked her back to her car, tucked her securely inside, and waved as she drove away. She couldn't be sure, because of the deep darkness of winter nights and the speed she maintained, but she could've sworn she saw flashes of navy blue and white now and then, following along beside her car in the sparse wooded areas at the sides of the roads. All the way home.

Chapter 9

She hungered. Her mouth moved, wanting to taste everything, but all her lips could grasp was air. Oddly enough, the whip of wind across her lips satisfied a deep need in her, a place she wasn't fully in touch with most days. She licked out, her tongue lashing the wind as it moved through her hair, caressed her body with invisible hands.

Lily turned as if weightless, suspended in air and time, grasping with her measly human hands to catch onto the wind. Pull it close to herself. Hold it dear. It slipped through her fingers again and again, soothing and stoking in equal measure.

"Boreas," she groaned, knowing without seeing as the scent of pine and wind wafted about her suspended body.

The voicing ended it all.

Lily startled awake, her own hoarse call waking her from the odd but delicious dream of the Greek god who'd stumbled into her small-town life. It took a minute, her breath still a heavy pant, for Lily to blink back to full wakefulness. Her fingers went to her cheeks, the heat there not wind-chap but lingering need.

She skimmed her hand from her cheek down, down, down, where she felt her own wetness pooled at the apex of her thighs. She cried out at her own touch, too sensitive from the dream.

Not too sensitive, actually, as she thought of Boreas and slowly stroked her clit. Primed and ready, a few circles, a few imaginings, and her legs shook from the force of her orgasm. However, it felt hollow. She didn't want her own fingers. She wanted wind and claw and the lips of a god.

Her thoughts were maudlin at best throughout the morning. She'd had something with Boreas the night before. He'd shown up for her. Done something directly asked of him. He'd proven himself to be a god of action in the face of her need.

He'd also stoked her desire. The alley scene replayed in her waking moments, so it was no surprise she'd filled in gaps with fantasies in her dreams. But she didn't want a fantasy. She wanted his warm body next to her, on her, and she was more than a little perturbed Ryan had interrupted all that could have been.

Because of all this, her morning had been a little more annoying than normal. Or, more aptly, she'd been annoyed by her typical morning more than usual.

She dragged her feet, muttered to herself, but did the same steps she did six days a week to open her shop. She double-checked inventory against sales, noting what she needed to make soon and what she could put off for a few more days. Busy season was busying for sure, so as soon as Isa showed that afternoon she needed to get to the back and crank out as many candles as she could. Until then, she could print out labels and such from her laptop in between customers.

Lucky for her, customers there were. From her official open at 9AM onward, she had a solid stream, including a bunch of tourists who'd been at the masquerade the night before who'd waited until they were about to leave town before they bought the bits and bobs they found from local artisans. She smiled, talked candles, sold a mass of them, and even gave out info on her Etsy shop and website, telling people to be on the lookout for what might come next. She'd been toying with the idea of doing seasonal candles more often, possibly every season. The success of her current Christmas release pushed her to think harder on the idea, and the notion of expansion.

Between two separate couples coming in to buy up taper candles for events they were throwing over the holiday season up in horse country—the very same tapers she'd dotted all over the streets of Holly Hollow the night before—she emailed Madison. If she became serious about her original dreams for growth – the idea of leaving Etsy for her own web sales and bringing on more help at the shop to fulfill orders and possibly give her a bit of a break –she had to discuss the issue with her accountant. Madison annoyed her, but she did her job well and would be upfront with her about options. Maybe even a little too upfront, but Lily needed the reality of snarky Madison before she fully committed to doing more with her business.

She paid herself enough to live a simple life. Paid Isa a good hourly wage well above the minimum in Kentucky. Covered her bills. Had plenty to funnel back into the business and keep a nice chunk of change in her business account just in case. All good things. Her uncertainty was whether she could effectively upscale her business, or if she'd plateaued into something sustainable and comfortable but never more. Lots to think on, and having someone dig into the reality of the numbers of it all would give those thoughts more concrete focus.

As she ruminated on what she might want to do with her life if she had a bit more time on her hands and freedom to produce and create, she thought of Boreas. Wondered what might be if he stopped hesitating so damn much. She wondered if she hesitated too much in everything. She never jumped right in with business, which was a good thing. Maybe she also hesitated too much with relationships, with what she desired.

One of the downsides of working alone for hours was Lily had a long time to think on what she wanted, what she could or couldn't do, how she may or may not be able to get to the life she wanted to live. She dug into the bubbling desire in her gut whenever she thought of Boreas. Considered the pull she felt toward the god. Finally, she wondered why she didn't simply reach out and grab what she wanted, like her hands had done with the wind in her dreams.

The ringing of another customer coming in the door brought her out of her thoughts. Wasn't a customer though. Lily spun to greet the person and came face-to-face with Ryan once again.

"What–?" she started, but didn't finish. Ryan, face hard and red with anger, stalked to her without a word and gripped her shoulders tight, giving her a quick shake.

"Who were you with last night?" he hissed out in her face.

Lily froze for a second, brought up short by Ryan's barely bottled rage.

Then her own anger rose to meet his. Instead of answering, she struggled, ripping herself from his grip with a massive wrench of her shoulders and stumbling away a few steps. He followed her close, step for step, and she flung up her hands to ward him off.

"Back off, Ryan," she yelled at him. "You have no right to touch me."

"You're mine, Lil."

She gave a mirthless laugh as she managed to get a center floor display between her and the angry man staring her down. "I ain't been yours for a good seven years, Ryan. What do you think has changed?"

"I'm back."

"And?"

He huffed and she wouldn't have been surprised if smoke spilled from his nostrils. "I came back here for you. To get back to where we were."

"Where we were? You mean when I lived oblivious to your cheating and you dragged me around wherever you wanted me to go, got me to do whatever you wanted me to do?"

"Now, Lil–" He stepped lightly then, as if about to explain. Placate. She was having none of it.

"No, Ryan. Breaking up came with some clarity. It wasn't simply that you cheated. You wanted me to be what you wanted me to be, which happened to be whatever helped you and your life. Never what made life better for me and mine."

"But I can give you a good life, Lil. Better than what you've had."

"What I've got is mine!" she yelled, her indignation pushing past her fear of this man in her shop. "Mine. I made it. With the help of some, including the lessons I learned from the likes of you. But mine all the same. You want to make it yours. Always did."

Ryan, in the face of her anger, ignored her points and brought the subject back to what he wanted, proving Lily's point, whether he realized it or not. "Who was the man you were with last night?"

"None of your damn business," she hissed back.

Again, he stepped forward, quick and aggressive, and again, Lily threw her arms up between them, landing them on his chest. He was muscled and toned, always had been, but he lacked the warmth and tingle she felt whenever she touched Boreas.

"You'll always be my business, baby."

Lily scuttled back then ran flat out, no longer caring. She grabbed her cordless as Ryan made his way behind her counter. He plucked it from her hand and tossed it on the counter behind him with a clatter of plastic. "Now, there's no need for that. Just answer the question, Lil."

"I did. I said 'None of your damn business.'"

His jaw clicked and ticked, tight and grinding. "You fucking him?"

She blinked. The absolutely absurdity of this incident made her laugh. Ryan started, enough for her to shove him back a few steps and gain some space.

"By the gods, Ryan, you are something else." She elbowed past him and snatched up the phone again, dialing 911 as she moved back to the middle of the room. He snatched the phone and flung it on the counter, the hit sounding like breaking plastic this time around. She wrenched her mouth to scream, at and about him, when the bell over the door sounded.

Lily half expected Betty. Not so. A slickly dressed Madison walked in, her high-heeled boots clicking on the pine. Lily used the distraction to put more space between her and Ryan, who'd lost some of the anger on his face at another person entering the shop.

"Madison," Ryan muttered, straightening his tie and his spine.

"Why, Ryan. Fancy seeing you here." She sucked her lips as she looked between Lily and the man she just wanted to go.

In fact.... "You need to leave, Ryan."

"Oh, don't let me interrupt two old lovebirds," Madison chirped.

"Leave. Now."

Ryan stared, shook himself from whatever thoughts he had, then plastered on a sly smirk for show. "We'll continue our conversation another time, Lil." He winked as he passed and said "Madison," in a slow, sexy drawl before he hit the bar on the door a little too hard and stomped away.

Lily sagged in relief before she looked back at Madison, who had her own hard smirk on her face. "You and Ryan getting back together?"

"God, no."

"Looked cozy to me," she said, taking the time to inspect her nails as if the answer meant nothing to her at all. It did. Lily knew it did. She'd seen Madison hanging on Ryan and laughing a touch too loud at his jokes the night before. Another thing she'd wanted to talk to her about besides business.

"Madison, there's nothing there with me and Ryan. Never will be. 'Cause he's bad news. You hear me?"

She laughed, "For you."

"No, Madison. For any woman. He's not a good man."

"And your secret admirer is?"

"Who?"

"That big hunk of a man you're with last night. Who was he, anyway?"

Far too many people had questions about Boreas now, and Lily was struck with the fact he'd been right to worry about how people might react. Not because he looked or acted different, at least not last night, but because they were in a small town where everyone stayed in everyone else's business. Still, she wanted to get through to Madison.

"Listen. It's not jealousy that has me saying this. Ryan isn't a good guy. You'd be better off steering clear."

Madison shrugged, and in an odd instance of not wanting to gossip, changed the subject. "You emailed about some financial questions?"

Lily nodded and allowed her the out. She might be a little too haughty and gossipy and such, but Lily did hope she watched herself.

The two moved behind the counter, where Lily started talking business once again. Madison did the same, her professional demeanor firmly in place, as they chatted growth opportunities for Lily's Lights.

She hoped there'd be a sign of Boreas that night when she closed shop. Nothing at her back door or at her house. Which had Lily itching to do something about it. She wanted him. He basically confessed he wanted her. Even went to lengths to get magic to help him do so. Why wait around after all that?

Chapter 10

The gray winter day barely penetrated the curtains in her front windows, making her even grumpier. Lily wasn't a morning person. Took her a bit to get up and at 'em, if she were honest with herself. She did it, pushed herself through morning face washing and teeth brushing and coffee until she felt a little more human each day. This Sunday, her one day off every week, was no exception. Maybe even worse, as a lot ran around her head.

Lily pushed herself too much. She felt exhaustion hovering. To keep up with the Christmas orders, she was working later and later every day, which was good and bad. Light appeared at the end of the tunnel, though. Christmas would come in a little over a week, which meant a full week shutdown until the new year. She'd given herself this one break every year since she opened the shop. Mostly because all the shops in downtown closed their shutters then so she didn't feel bad following suit.

Another bright spot: her chat with Madison post-Ryan went well. She talked hard numbers, realistic ways to move forward, and gave Lily her unvarnished professional opinion: if this quarter ended as she projected, she saw no issue with Lily slowly expanding. Once the quarterly numbers were tallied, her first order of business was hiring another sales associate to help out, at least part time, during the day. Her second required hiring someone to revamp her website and add a web store, so she could say goodbye to those pesky Etsy rules and fees. It'd be awful nice to do things the way she wanted to do them and not have to give someone else her money for the privilege.

All good, but it didn't help her current weariness. Which, to be honest, could be from fretting over what Ryan would do next. Or the fact Boreas hadn't shown his face, or left any surprises, since they kissed on Wednesday night. She thought they'd worked it all out, but something still held him back. She stewed over all of it.

On that thought, as if conjured by her annoyance, the phone on her wall rang. Lily sighed, knowing exactly who it would be. Everyone else used her cell. Not Ryan. Not when he wanted to be a pain in her ass. She ignored it. Until about the eighth ring. She stomped around her small fire, slammed her coffee cup down a little too hard on her counter, and whipped the receiver out of its cradle.

"What do you want today, Ryan?" she huffed into the phone.

Nothing. Of fucking course.

She was done. With all of it. With Ryan being an ass at every opportunity. With Boreas refusing to acknowledge the connection between them and running scared. Done.

"Look here, ass. I'm hanging up and calling the sheriff. Getting a restraining order, like I should've done years ago but didn't, because you were scared shitless of Michael. I'm not waiting for my brother to roll back into town, so you're going to stop some other way."

A soft chuckle hit her ear before silence. The dial tone blared in her ear before she slammed the headpiece back into its cradle.

"Damnit all to hell," she yelled and stomped, trying to get her anger out in some way.

She did just what she told Ryan she'd do. She grabbed her cell and called the sheriff's office to ask about a restraining order. Lily learned why he chuckled–it took far too much to get one. Apparently, because he hadn't physically hurt her—yet—they couldn't do anything about it. She could file a report and request, they told her, but seeing as Ryan was a lawyer, they doubted a judge would grant it unless he physically assaulted her.

Cursing the ridiculous way the law always seemed to fail women, she seethed for a good few minutes until her mind turned to the other male annoyance in her life. Boreas. Ryan freaked her out. Boreas just needed a swift kick in the pants.

Lily mumbled to herself about stubborn men as she pulled on a thick sweater, fleece-lined leggings, her big puffy coat, and her wool hat and gloves. She stomped into her hiking boots, pausing to think about how the last time she wore them she hurt her ankle down in the hollow. Shaking the idea away, she grabbed her keys and motored out the door, not once thinking to check the weather or consider the dark clouds gathered in the distance.

She huddled into herself as much as she could, curled around her body to conserve warmth as she hunkered down behind a jutting rock. She'd cursed men earlier, but now cursed herself for a fool. Lily shivered, stuck in a damn snowstorm, lost in the woods somewhere around the Daniel Boone National Forest, and it wasn't looking good for her.

She'd gone tearing out of her house, driving a little too quickly to the place where she'd first met Boreas. Fueled by annoyance and desire, she made her way to the hollow, ignoring the small flakes of snow when they first started to dust the ground. Soon enough, however, the dusting became a flurry and the flurry became a downpour, and she found herself trudging through snow as she followed the creek deeper and deeper into the forest in search of the wind god.

"Idiot," she said aloud to herself, about herself, as her teeth chattered. Before she knew it, her path back became obscured by falling snow. She might have gotten turned around, and the snow made everything too blurry to notice how or where or when. She'd never come across the rock before she leaned against it to help break the wind, she knew that much.

Shivering, she closed her eyes, trying to move her hands quickly up and down her arms to get more warmth there. Lily wasn't in danger. Yet. If she didn't find her way out of the forest, though, it might be touch and go. In the deep woods, where light barely existed in winter, the sun set quickly this time of year. The cold set in even quicker.

God, she'd done something similar only weeks before. Even thought on it when she put on her boots that morning. Determined to make a man face her and his issues, she ignored it.

Didn't think straight. She laughed to herself, mirthless, thinking she might just deserve it for trying to force something from a man who didn't seem to want it. Or, at least, didn't want it enough.

Her granny would've blistered her butt for the stupidity she'd shown every step of the way.

Pushing her head into her knees, she turned her cheek as a particularly hard wind flowed over her head. She thought of him then, of his smell, and she whispered his name into the wind, layers of frustration and need mingling dark and heavy in her voice.

Her eyes closed for a good three or four minutes, then she took a deep, cold breath to shake herself out of her self-pity once again and figure a way out (once again), when she heard a growled call rip through the sky. "LILY!"

She'd recognize his voice anywhere, even though she'd literally heard it only a handful of times. Lily found her feet and turned her face to the sky. "Here, Boreas. Over here!"

Lily waved her arms around blindly because she couldn't see more than a few feet in front of her face. Then the god appeared almost out of nowhere, feathered wings flapping in the snowy sky, his face hard and as cold as the wind around them. He looked unhappy to say the least.

He said not a word as he landed. Boreas grabbed her by the shoulder, looking over her body to make sure she wasn't injured. When he seemed satisfied she appeared well and mostly whole, he hooked his head up toward the sky, a silent question she somehow understood. Nodding yes, she gasped slightly when he scooped her up in his arms, cradling her behind her knees and shoulders, and shot off into the sky.

She was too cold, too relieved, too nervous to take it all in. Not to mention all the snow. Her heart thumped hard at the warmth of Boreas around her and the idea of them flying in the sky together. Sadly, it didn't last long. Boreas landed with a thud in front of a large cave opening, and without a word, headed into the dark recesses with Lily still in his arms.

Lily knew she'd been stupid. Reckless. More than once. A lot more than once if she thought back on her life. She got a wild hair and ran, not often thinking of consequences. Now, despite her shivers and the anger etched in Boreas's face, she fleetingly thought it worked out all right in the end this time. Because she stood inside Boreas's home.

Couldn't exactly call it a house because it was deep in a cave. They'd travelled a good lick down into the dark recesses, the walls coming in closer and closer until the god squeezed them sideways through a small opening that led into a big, bright, warm, cavernous room. The ceilings high above their heads held beautifully formed stalactites, varying shades of earthy brown flowing down and frozen in place like icicle chandeliers above them. A few stalagmites peppered the floor, some glistening off white like they were made of gypsum or some other cave crystal.

Intermixed with the natural wonder of the place were modern conveniences. A crammed bookcase stood by an overstuffed leather chair and ottoman seated on a beautiful, intricate, thick rug in the center of the room. Off to one side was a large fireplace, roaring with orange and yellow flames. All kinds of cooking utensils she'd seen in her school visits to living history frontier towns hung beside it: a large kettle on a turning hook that could easily be pushed into or pulled out of the fire, a toaster, a long-handled pan. A massive platform stretched across the far wall, piled with covers and pillows in a comfy mishmash. Had to be his bed.

"I like your space," she said, turning in a circle to take it all in.

When he didn't reply, she stopped to face him. He stood as still and firm as the stalagmites on his floor, arms folded and hard as stone. His face remained cold, and then she noticed the odd swirling of dust and cave bits around him, as if his wind was picking up speed and force, becoming a mini cyclone.

Lily cocked her head. "Boreas?"

She didn't get to get anything else out, because he exploded with a gale force that whipped her hair back. "What the fuck were you thinking?"

Lily blinked in the face of his anger. "I came to see you," she said, her voice small. She knew she'd done wrong. Hadn't thought it all out. Then again, she wouldn't have had to do it if Boreas hadn't kept doing this cryptic disappearing act.

On that thought, she straightened and faced off with the god. "Because you couldn't be bothered to talk to me like a damn adult."

His lip curled in answer, a soft growl came up his throat, and the soft light in the cavern glinted off his wicked canines, but Lily had no fear. Felt no need to defend herself physically. No. Instead, she would give him a piece of her mind.

"What? You thought I'd just wait around for you? Pine like some silly girl, begging for whatever scraps you'd give me?"

The questions echoed as he stared in shock and dawning understanding. "Lily," he said, stepping closer then stopping himself, his wind dying down along with his anger.

"No. Don't say 'Lily' in that way that sounds like you're winding up for some lecture on how the silly human doesn't understand the ways of gods. Maybe I don't. Maybe I don't know what it is to be a god, but you don't know what it is to be a human woman, either. To feel what I feel and be left high and dry every single time. I thought we'd gotten past this, then you don't come see me for days."

"I did not..."

"Because you're a scaredy cat."

"Excuse me?" His voice hit low, menacing, in her ears but she ignored it.

"You heard me loud and clear. Big, bad god of wind terrified of little old me. Despite knowing we should be together. Hell, the book proved that weeks ago."

"Do you think me unaware of this fact?" He yelled, stepping closer, no longer stopping himself. "I attempted to give you space, even if I have no quarter in my own mind. You are everywhere for me. In my nose. Under my skin. Invading my dreams."

"I don't want space, and I thought I made that point pretty damn clear Wednesday night. All I want is you."

"You remain unaware of all we are, and what being together may mean."

Stepping closer to him, making the distance between them mere inches, Lily pushed into his face, wrapping her arms around his shoulders. "I don't know anything about magic, and frankly, I don't care. I feel you everywhere. Think of you all the time. Dream of you touching me. I ache for you, Boreas. Please, help me stop the ache. That's all I ask."

His eyes closed a fraction of a second then opened wide, their icy depths a piercing glow in the dark cave. "As you wish," he said right before he slammed his lips against her own.

Chapter 11

Boreas's kiss seared her cold lips, a shock of lust roaring to life in an instant. His mouth, firm and insistent, worked against her own, and all she could do was take what he gave. She felt the scrape of his large canine along the seam of her mouth, and she gasped at the current it sent directly to her core. He pressed the advantage, thrusting his tongue into her mouth. She'd never fully understood the idea of a kiss plundering, something she read often in her most-loved romance novels, until this moment. His tongue took everything she gave and demanded more, each stroke and dip causing her to give him more of herself, meeting his demand with her own need.

She leaned into his arms, then melted into them, and with a whirl of wind, her back hit something soft. He ripped his head away on a deep growl and she blinked her eyes to take in their change of position. They were on his platform bed, her arms flung up over her head. Her body stretched beneath him like an offering as he trapped her with his own strong arms planted beside her shoulders.

Boreas's face, always gorgeous, looked ethereal. A glint of white light came from his eyes, casting an eerie glow over his face, making the sharp lines and swooping curves starker in the darker corners of the cave. Lily lifted her hand to trace his cheekbone. "Beautiful," she whispered.

The light blinked out of his eyes. "No, Lily. I am no beauty. I am not even human. I am a monster, something humans feared long ago when they knew of me." As if to emphasize his confession, he curled his lips to expose his wickedly sharp teeth and tapped the downy cover of the bed with one pointed claw.

Lily turned, grabbed his hand, and brought it to her lips, kissing each of his clawed tips in turn, caressing the jagged cliffs and valleys of the large knuckle. "Beautiful," she repeated. Not on a whisper, but with firm surety.

He hung his head for a moment and when his eyes came back to her, the light returned with a blaze. He said no more, simply pressed down and took her mouth before trailing kisses down her cheeks, her neck. Boreas paused, a shuddered breath on his lips, as if asking something. Lily, more than ready, jostled to give herself some space to get undressed.

"Allow me," he said as she struggled out of her puffer. Boreas urged her to stand and he moved around, sweeping her hair aside and kissing the back of her neck before he began. He first gently removed her hat, placing it on a nightstand beside them. Her coat came next, and she felt his claws skim her arms even through her layers, causing her breath to stutter out in a disjointed hiss of pleasure. Next came her sweater, swept over her head in a quick flutter. Then her thermal shirt, and she cursed the fact she layered up so much before heading out the door that morning.

The only thing left on her torso was her serviceable white t-shirt bra. She didn't have time to consider what lingerie might have been better because the sear of his strong hands on her shoulders took all thought from her head.

Boreas gripped her a moment, his hands so large his fingers skimmed more than halfway down the white straps on the front of her shoulders. So large she easily saw them, olive skin gleaming. Pointed claws pressed against pale skin and the thinnest strip of white fabric. A growl rumbled behind her and Boreas said "Lily," as if in warning. As if he could smell the wetness such a sight caused.

His breath feathered her shoulder, dotting sucking kisses there as he gripped her tight. His hands pulled her back to his chest, and she felt his nakedness there. A pouty whimper sounded when his hands left her shoulders, then she felt a gentle tap at her calf. He went foot by foot, undoing then removing her hiking boots and socks.

Those impressive hands came up the outsides of her legs slowly as he rose, until they snagged in the tops of leggings. She wiggled her butt when he hesitated and with a masculine, knowing chuckle, he began another descent to the floor, taking her leggings with him. Again, he ascended, but kisses marked his progress. Gentle nips and licks followed, all the way back to her shoulders.

A gentle wind caressed her body as his hands turned her so they were face to face. The hunger she saw when she locked eyes with him again mirrored the need she felt in her own gut, the pull she felt toward him that had to be obeyed. "Boreas," she gasped out, a plea for more.

He hushed her and fell back, slowed by a breeze so they landed gingerly on the bed, her body finally making full contact with his own. He still had on underwear. She knew because she didn't feel the heat of his flesh as acutely where her thighs met his shorts. Boreas held her tight a moment before he flipped them, laying her on the bed as he hovered. His wings flared above them both, a feathery canopy she wanted to touch. It was no time to deny herself, so she reached out and traced a sharp feather with a finger. A shudder wracked his impressive frame and she moved her hand from wing to strong shoulder to chest to flexing abs to the very edge of a maddeningly tight pair of boxer briefs.

Boreas stopped her progress, his claws indenting the flesh on her hand. "Not yet. I need a taste." He pushed her hand above her head and she instinctively added her other. With one massive, clawed hand he held both her wrists above her head and kissed his way down her body. Mouth, cheek, neck, upper chest. Between kisses, his deep voice rang out "Do you like this?" He nipped one white strap of her bra to clarify his question and she shook her head no. His second hand came up and with one sharp tip, he ripped through the cloth between her breasts, freeing them from the fabric confines.

Like most woman in her thirties, her breasts followed gravity once freed. Boreas followed with his lips and free hand, taking one in a firm grip and the other in his mouth. She moaned loudly, and once the wave of pleasure at the first hot contact ebbed enough for her to think, she couldn't clearly decide which she liked better: the wet scrape of his teeth as he sucked one puckered nipple in his mouth or the dry scrape of a claw as his hand alternately kneaded her aching breast and tweaked her nipple.

He seemed lost in a haze, focused solely on the task in front of him. Lily's pleasure rose and rose, her body squirming under his ministrations. But she needed more. She ached with need, one leg curling around his torso so she could grind her pussy against his hard body.

Boreas ripped his lips away, teeth flashing from the light in his eyes. "Lily," he warned once again, but she ignored it.

She arched up, grinding against him harder, and said only one word again. A final, need-filled plea to give them both what they wanted. What they needed. "Please."

He gave a swift kiss to the expanse of skin on her chest and knifed up in a whoosh, his wings helping suspend him for a few beats. Lily came up on her elbows to watch. One clawed hand rubbed the massive bulge in his boxer briefs as he licked his lips and stared at the plain white bikini briefs she wore. He didn't ask then, he simply shot out one claw and tore through those panties like they were made of paper. Her breath hitched at the act just as he muttered out "fuck" at the sight of Lily fully naked in front of him for the first time.

The god moved in a blur, and before she knew it, he towered over her, fully naked and stroking his cock. She stared, because his cock looked unlike anything she'd ever seen. The basic shape was similar to a human man's penis, she supposed. It also matched his olive skin tone. Except for the ice-white swirls and ridges running all around it in a cyclone pattern. Those delicious looking patterns rose from his thick root, working up to the large, rounded tip, almost like a ribbed condom designed with gales of wind in mind. She thought of the phrase "ribbed for her pleasure" and gave a soft giggle. Lily licked her lips, echoing Boreas's own actions mere seconds before.

He slowly climbed on top of her, bending deep to kiss the swell of her stomach, her chest, her cheek. "Ready?" he asked, stroking himself once again as he looked over her face. She lay there breathless, speechless, needy, so she nodded her head yes.

He'd positioned himself between her legs. With one strong hand he gripped her hip and raised it from the bed. With the other he guided his cock right to the heart of her. When his head notched against her pussy she sucked in a breath. He waited a beat then thrust forward, hitting true and deep in one smooth stroke.

Lily cried out in pleasure. Boreas breathed out a moan, his eyes squeezed tight as if he couldn't handle so much sensation all at once. Lily understood the feeling.

Slowly, he pulled free, and she felt every ridge in his large, beautiful, swirling cock as he did. A pause, then another thrust, again hitting a spot inside her no one before had reached. She half came off the bed, and with his free hand he pushed her chest down, pinning her to the bed as he thrust into her over and over again, his steady beat a hard and fast rhythm.

"Fuck," he breathed out as he slammed into her and ground hard, hitting her clit and causing Lily to let out another long moan. "Perfect. You're fucking perfect for me. Fit me so well."

She agreed, but with his steady thrust and grind, her breath came in hard pants, so she simply met his hips with her own. He dipped down to take her mouth. Moans, groans, growls, the slick slap of flesh on flesh filled the open cavern of his home, echoing off the dark walls and bouncing back at them as they lost themselves in each other's bodies.

Soon enough, her pleasure reached a breaking point. He felt it of course, and began to speak. However, the words sounded harsh, more garbled, more slurred, as if he couldn't quite get them out around his bared fangs. "Lily. Come for me. Come around me while I am buried inside you. Right fucking now." He slid the hand at her chest down, and one sharp claw flicked against her clit.

Lily detonated, a fierce orgasm ripping through her body like a bomb, shattering her in its wake. She felt undone. In pieces. The coursing pleasure left her shaking and spent.

Boreas, as if he'd held back before, pounded harder and faster into her, groaning, "Yes, fuck yes," as he did, until he planted himself deep. She felt his large cock twitch as he came, his head flung back and his wings shaking above them both.

He sagged, letting her hip drop as he slowly pulled out of her, and went back on his knees so he knelt above her. His hands met on her stomach and fanned outward, as if he wanted to caress every inch of her. Wind followed his touch, giving a soft swirl over her flesh, helping her body ease. After long minutes, Lily began to squirm.

"Um, Boreas. Is there a bathroom here?"

He'd been staring down, watching his hands roam her body, and at her words his head snapped up. "Are you okay, my flower?"

He hadn't called her any type of nickname before, and something burrowed into her heart at the newness of it. "Just peachy. I need to pee, though. Maybe clean up."

"Of course." He stood, not at all caring about his nakedness, and scooped her up like he had before. It'd been snug and lovely then, but felt far more delicious when they were naked.

In a few quick strides, they were around the bed and at a nook in the wall she hadn't noticed before. He eased them through a small, tight hallway until they reached a bathing chamber. There was a place to use the bathroom, but it wasn't like a modern toilet. A box-like structure came up from the floor, with a hinge at the top and a lever at the sides. She looked at it in confusion and before she could ask, he explained. "Pressurized water used as an ancient flusher before modern plumbing." He pointed to the lever. "Lift the lid, do what you will, lower the lid and pull the lever. The process will take care of the rest."

She looked at a small circular chamber with another lever and box system suspended from the ceiling. "Shower?" She asked.

He smiled and nodded before moving aside and pointing to the sink-like setup behind him. He reached over to a shelf and handed her a towel. "Take your time. Use whatever you need." She smiled and he left her to it.

She didn't take long, but she came back feeling relieved and cleaner. Her mind did a record scratch when she saw Boreas stretched out in the middle of his large bed, laying on his feather wings, large biceps flexed with his hands up under his head. His dark covers were pulled up to his waist, leaving his expansive chest on full display.

He smiled and pulled up the covers as she walked his way. "Come," he said, and a memory of him using a similar word as a different command only minutes before made her insides liquid. His nose flared, and his smile turned to a smirk.

Lily climbed in, ignoring the look he gave her, and snuggled deep into his chest. "Mmmm. Warm."

He didn't reply. Boreas slipped his arms around her, followed by the curve of his wings, and enveloped her in his warm pine and breeze scent. In less than a minute, she fell asleep, content in his godly embrace.

Chapter 12

Lily woke wrapped in warm arms and feathers a touch too sharp. Plastered against Boreas's chest, she raised her cheek slowly, hesitant from sleep and not wanting to wake the god in bed with her. She knew she failed when the softest of breezes ruffled her hair and she heard "My flower," whispered from above her head.

Giving up the ghost, she planted her hands in his chest to push herself up and stare down into his impossibly gorgeous face. "Hey," she said, soft and slightly shy. Why she'd be shy now, after what they'd done before, she couldn't quite say, except this somehow felt more intimate.

One wing curled up and scraped against her face. It wasn't an unpleasant sensation, but strange to see a feather and feel the unusual edge of it. The question popped from her mouth before she could swallow it. "Why are your feathers so different?"

He withdrew his wing quickly, pulling into himself, and she halted him, laying a hand on the underside of his wingspan. He practically purred at her touch, and the tension in his body after her question eased a touch. "I'm not saying I don't like it, Boreas. I'm just wondering."

His ice blue eyes roved over her face before he answered. "There is no real reason I can explain, except to say they are as I am."

Lily nodded her head, lost in the thought of gods, and stuffed down the questions she had about godly evolutionary biology. Easy to shrug it off with a whispered "magic." For now.

He chuckled and spun them in the sheets, a soft, warm breeze floating around them. Cocooning them. One claw traced the curve of her cheek, stopping at the dimple at the side of her mouth. "Magic," he repeated, and a soft blow hit her gut, knocking the wind from her.

Because she was who she was, she shook it off and laughed. "Well, this magician needs some water."

Boreas jumped out of the bed in a flash she couldn't track, rustling around in an old-school metal kitchen cabinet beside the fireplace, gloriously naked. He muttered something she didn't get, so she rose from the bed as she wrapped the sheet around her like her own toga and asked "huh?" His head popped up out of the cabinet and he gripped a plastic bottle of water when he asked, "Do you mind room temperature?"

Rubbing her hands up and down her arms, she chuckled. "Room temp ain't all that high right now, so sure."

The god's face fell and he moved, taking only a handful of steps to reach her. He scooped her up, his favorite way to move her about apparently. She snuggled close and spoke into his chest. "It's fine, Boreas." He gave a deep huff in reply before he adjusted her in his leather reading chair and went to the fireplace. In moments, it roared to life. The flaming heat hit her face, warming her. Not as warming as the god's broad chest, but still nice.

She snuggled into the chair, taking the time to look around his little reading area. "Not big on TV?"

"Television is acceptable, even entertaining at times," he said, placing the water bottle he dug up for her on the small table beside the chair. "The cave does not have great reception."

"Ah." Reaching for the water, her hand halted at what she saw next to it. There, right by an old leather book, sat one of her candles. This year's Christmas candle to be exact. Instead of lifting the water to her mouth, she hefted the candle in the air and waved it at Boreas with a wide grin. "When'd you get this?"

Something like a blush crept over the god's bronze face, but he tamped it down so quick she wasn't sure she saw it. "I ordered it as soon as you put it online."

"I thought there wasn't much service here?" She teased.

He crossed his arms over his chest and with a grumble said, "I have a smartphone, Lily, and I do know how to use it."

Her face closed down at his quip. "Do you now?"

He leaned in front of her in a blink, placing the candle back on the table as he knelt. "Yes, Lily. However, there are reasons I never used it with you directly."

"Oh, really?" She meant to be blasé but a hint of hurt lingered in her tone.

Without looking, he snapped up the leather book at their side and waved it between them. Only then did she notice it was *Book of Desires*. "When'd you get this from the shop?"

"I didn't. It lay here, by my chair, when I awoke this morning."

"Magic," she said once again.

"Yes, Lily. Yes." He sighed, deep and long, before sitting back on his heels to look her full in the face. "I told you only bits and pieces of the legend of this book. Nothing specific. Nothing of what I did with it.

"Years ago, before I came to this forest, I wandered for centuries, until I found this in an old, crowded bookshop in Istanbul." He rubbed his forehead as if the memory pained him. "I'd wandered a long time, Lily. I grew tired and lonely. Knowing what I found, I did the unthinkable. I used it."

"Why is that unthinkable? Ain't it supposed to be used? It's a spell book after all. Spells are meant to be cast."

"Yes, but magic can be tricky. Spell magic even more so, which is why there are few true witches in the world. The one who made this was trained by Hecate herself, in the English wilderness, long after the fall of the gods. She connected it to godhood specifically. Hecate claimed it was to help with our loneliness, help us find what we needed after our loss of rule, but many feared what it might do, just as they feared what humans might do if they remembered gods walked among them. The vampires, the werewolves, the witches, they stayed apart from but a part of the human world after their bloody fight to be recognized and known. We gods chose to disappear, retreat, fade from memory, after the violence and bloodshed that ensued when humans discovered we were vulnerable in certain regards. We, as a group, thought to stay hidden, rather than bring more violence down on our heads. Because humans are so very good at violence when they are faced with the previously unknown."

Lily thought about werewolves and vampires and the mysteries people believed every day, but she didn't say anything. He had a healthy dose of fear for a very real and very harsh, reason, and she wouldn't push him on it. Instead, she silently encouraged him to continue his story.

He flung open the book and it flipped as if by itself, turning quickly from page to page until it landed on a certain spell. "Here, Lily. This is what I called forth."

Lily leaned closer to read the page but she still couldn't read Latin. She knew some conversational Spanish, a smattering of French, but Latin had never seemed useful for someone not looking to be a doctor or lawyer. More fool her, she supposed.

"I can't read this," she said, leaning back.

"It's a spell to find purpose, Lily. That's what I asked the book for. Not wealth or prosperity or love. Above all else, I wanted a reason to keep on living." The last bit, the important bit, came out in a harsh whisper and smashed Lily right in the face. Tears welled in her eyes.

"I performed the spell, as instructed, and found myself here, in this forest, seven years ago. I wasn't looking for love, but when I met you, I knew who you were. What you were. I knew my purpose. To protect you. Even from myself."

"I don't need protection," she pushed and he held his hands up in surrender.

"I know. I know, Lily. I simply thought..."

"Thought what?"

"You'd be better off if I stayed in the shadows, helped from a distance. It would be enough for me, to watch over you and give you what you needed, when you needed."

"Once we met, what I needed most was *you*," Lily said. Maybe a touch too harshly.

He hung his head and clasped her hand. "Please, forgive me, Lily. I thought I knew best. Instead of talking with you, learning from you yourself, I kept us apart, when what we are makes that impossible."

"What are we?"

He leaned forward and kissed her cheek. "Mates," he answered on her skin, his breath a chilly wind causing goosebumps to raise all over her body.

Lily started at the word. She knew it, of course. Little common knowledge about werewolves and vampires existed outside a few hard facts. One of those facts: the lucky ones had fated mates, which were the most precious thing anyone in their culture could find.

"What does it mean for us?"

Boreas pulled back once again, looked down between them, and stretched out a clawed finger to trace something there. Lily felt it in her gut, where the connection tugged at her. Her eyes flared. He could feel it too, somehow *touch* it.

"It means I am yours, forever. As you are mine. Especially now we have joined our flesh. We are fated to be together in this world, by whatever makes such things happen. Perfectly compatible."

"But you're so frustrating!" She slapped her hadn't over her mouth in embarrassment, but that didn't mean her statement wasn't true.

Boreas laughed, loud as a crack of lightning in a winter storm. "I am certain I am, my flower." He scooped her up yet again and rearranged them so she sat on his lap in the chair. He turned her so she could look up into his face as he pushed a stray strand of brown hair behind her ear. "I assure you, I will continue to be, on occasion. However, a little back and forth makes for interesting times...." He trailed off, looking back at the bed, and Lily remembered what they felt like together. Explosive. Undeniable. Life-changing.

She harrumphed, as if she'd made some valid point, when she'd not said a word, then smiled his way. "You learned your lesson, then? No more fighting this mate business?"

He countered with his own question. "You do not mind this revelation... amongst so many revelations?"

She took the time to think on his question. A lot of new things had tumbled into her life in a short span of time: gods, magic, mates. However, she didn't mind at all. Maybe because she apparently came made for this, for him. She'd sensed a binding to him since meeting the god and had never questioned it. Lily figured she shouldn't start doing so, once he'd explained it all. "I guess we both are as we are made: to be with one another. So, no, I don't mind. Got it? No more hesitating or badgering me about it, alright?"

"Yes, ma'am."

"Huh. Ma'am. Don't know if I like that."

Boreas nuzzled into her neck, causing her breath to catch. "Do you like 'flower'?"

She nodded because she couldn't speak with the god licking and nipping her neck.

"Good girl," he growled in her ear.

"I like that, too," she managed to choke out.

He grabbed her chin and gave her a long, hard kiss before he ripped his face away, forcing himself to stop. "Water," he said. He'd care for her even at his own expense. As was his purpose.

Lily fake pouted, but she was pretty dang thirsty, so she took the bottle when he handed it to her. He sat there holding her tight until she drank the whole thing down. Lily didn't complain, though. Not when his heat and care wrapped around her like tinsel on a Christmas tree.

Chapter 13

He flew her back to her car at twilight, after Lily said she wanted to go home to change, shower, get ready for work in the morning. All the responsible adult things she didn't want to do but needed to do. No, she wanted to stay in his cave and sate their lust all night if possible. Yet, she did what she had to do. Her Granny's sense of obligation and responsibility ran deep. Deeper than her lust, apparently.

Once there, they discovered a new problem: snow covered the car, and the tires looked half buried as well. It'd quit coming down some time before. She couldn't say when, what with spending the bulk of the day deep in Boreas's cave. She thought at least it wasn't snowing then. Soon enough, she learned of a secondary perk of being with a god of the wind.

Boreas blew most of the loose snow away. Even used his wings and impressive muscles to clear the snow around her tires. The gravel road where she'd parked was covered pretty good, too, but Boreas sent a heavy wind in front as they drove to sweep it from their path. Lily smiled, wide and joyful, humming along to the soft strains of the local AM bluegrass station.

Boreas bobbed his head along, reaching over at one point to grip her thigh and smile her way. It sent a thrill up her back, and

Lily wondered if this feeling would ever go away, after years and years together. Maybe too early to think in terms of years, but they were fated mates. Seemed to imply forever to her.

They moved down the gravel road, the country highway, all the way to Lily's small house on the edges of town in companionable silence except for the twang of banjos and the mad slide of fiddles. Her long driveway twisted around a few clusters of trees dotting her large front yard before her small house popped up on top of a hill, far from the road. Of course, snow buried any view of her driveway. Not for long, though. Boreas flicked a hand as if shooing the snow away, and his wind whipped ahead, clearing the path easily.

When they reached the small carport attached to the side of her house, she noticed the snow tumbling off the sidewalk to her front door and laughed out loud. "You're going to save me a good bit of money in snow removal, Boreas."

Once outside the car, his wings spread, a mass of sharp white feathers rising above them both, so tall they brushed the roof of the carport. They beat one, two, three times, each movement causing more wind to blow. The small drifts of snow still on the ground floated upward with his wind, as if falling in reverse. With a flick of his clawed hand high in the air, the lip of snow hanging precariously from her carport gutters tumbled down, mixing with his winds and the ground snow, creating a pretty, powdery mini cyclone behind her car. It twirled until he tucked in his wings tight to his back. But not before she gave a joyful laugh at the sight. He'd given her a ballet of snow, and it was beautiful to watch.

Boreas turned to her, flashing his fangs with a wide smile, and said, "Shall we?" His arm came out and she took his elbow at the crook, allowing him to walk her up the sidewalk he cleared and to her snow-free doorstep.

Once inside her small entryway, they each shook off the tiny remnants of snow clinging to them. Lily unbundled. Boreas wore his usual uniform of a toga and not much else. Apparently the god of North Wind didn't need to keep himself from getting hypothermia.

"Have a seat," she said, gesturing to her couch. "I'm going to call my snow removal guy real quick. Tell him I don't need his services this time."

"Tell him you won't be needing his services in the future," Boreas rumbled her way.

She dipped her head down to look at her cell. As she typed in the first few letters of Guy's name to pull up his contact, the phone on her kitchen wall rang. Lily's shoulders tensed instantly. Boreas noticed.

Walking slowly into the kitchen, she hoped with every step it'd just stop before she reached the damned thing. Sadly, it didn't. Lily took a deep breath and felt Boreas's warmth at her back when she lifted the headpiece off the cradle. "Hello?" Maybe it'd be someone else.

"Who the fuck is with you Lily?"

Her eyes widened. How in the hell did Ryan know about Boreas being in her house? She looked around, frantic for a moment, fear causing her heart to beat heavy and hard in her chest.

Boreas took the phone from her and put it to his ear. "Who is this?" he asked, his voice a vicious bite. A beat of silence passed on Boreas's end, but she could hear Ryan, tinny to her ears, so she couldn't exactly make out what he yelled. The idea of Boreas being exposed to Ryan's rants made her angry on his behalf, helping her melt away some of her fear and shift it to anger. Without another word, she reached up and slammed it down in the cradle, cutting off Ryan's voice.

Boreas seethed, inches away from her, but she didn't feel the pit of fear she felt whenever Ryan became angry in her presence. "Your ex?"

She nodded. "He..." She didn't know what to say about him. He seemed more and more unhinged. "He knows you're here... in all that is you." That felt like the most pressing place to start.

Boreas muscles tensed, his eyes narrowed, and a hard, sharp huff like the rumble of bear sounded. He held up a hand to get her to stay right where she stood and moved through the kitchen, living room, entryway, his icy blue eyes searching. He flung open her front door, and she supposed he searched around there. Minutes later he came back with a crushed piece of tech in his hand. It looked to be a small camera.

"Your carport," he growled, and Lily got sick to her stomach at the thought of Ryan watching her for who knew how long.

"Stay here," he actually said this time, moving into the other rooms of the house, checking each before he returned to her. "There are no other cameras."

A bit of good news for Lily, so she sagged in relief. Boreas, however, remained stiff and unmoving. "You did not tell me you were having... issues with your ex."

"I didn't."

"Do you not think that is something I should know?" His arms crossed on his chest. Still, she felt no fear when she met him toe-to-toe.

"When was I supposed to do that? While you were running away from me as fast as your wings could carry you? Hmmm?"

His anger deflated, a chilly wind whirled around them, and he swept her up in a deep, warm hug. "I apologize. You are correct." A heavy sigh, then, "I know now, and we will handle it. Together."

She was glad he wasn't about to fly off and find Ryan. Rip him limb from limb or something. Not because Ryan didn't deserve it, but Boreas wanted to remain hidden, and a bloody trail like that wasn't exactly conducive to not letting the townspeople know who and what you were. Townspeople of any era tended to frown on one of their own getting ripped apart by an unknown creature, even if the one of their own turned out to be a total ass.

"Okay. Okay. I need a drink. And we need to talk. You want something?" He nodded and she asked if wine sounded okay before she poured them both a big glass of red she had lying around. They moved to the couch. She told him about Ryan. Everything from their past to what he'd been doing since he moved back a month or so ago.

"Boreas,"—she rested an arm on his now clenched, clawed hand—"he's vindictive and petty. Maybe it's best for you to take some time away, let his anger blow over." Ryan couldn't do anything to the god physically. He could, however, cause them a whole mess of trouble in other ways, and he'd do it, when it best served him to do so.

The god shook his head. "No, my flower. I'm here, in my purpose. I will not leave you."

"But..." she wanted to protect him, shield him from what might come his way with Ryan's craziness.

"No, Lily. I will stay. Face whatever this Ryan has in store for us. With you. As we determined already."

They had already had this talk, one where she had to convince him. Now he convinced her. She supposed she couldn't fall down at the first hurdle, so she nodded in agreement.

By this time, it was closing in on seven. She looked down at herself and grimaced. "Yikes. I need a shower."

The worry left Boreas's eyes and white heat flashed there. "You have a very nice shower," he cooed at her. "Roomy."

Lily leaned into him. "I like roomy showers. They can be an awful lot of fun."

He growled and scooped her into his arms as he rose from the couch. She laughed, worry melting away behind the lust pounding in her blood.

When he slid her down his body, they stood a hair's width apart in her bathroom, both breathing so heavy their chests brushed with each inhale. His eyes, the odd white light coming back to them in a softer glow, skimmed her from head to toe. A heft of breath, and he hovered a large, clawed hand over her shoulders. She wavered on her feet, leaning even more into him, an invitation.

Boreas gripped her throat suddenly, and Lily felt the scrape of claws all the way at the back of her neck. The grip wasn't hard or menacing but forceful enough to have her heart pump in overdrive with a heady mix of lust and uncertainty. Not fear, though. Never fear with him, despite those claws on her neck.

With a large, strong thumb, he moved her chin left and right, as if studying her face up close for the first time. "Magnificent," he whispered before he bent down to plant a soft kiss on her lips. The kiss ramped up her need, her want, and her thighs rubbed together in response. The one wicked claw at her chin thumped it hard, the tip digging slightly into her flesh, before he tilted her face up so she looked straight at the ceiling.

Boreas bent further down, moving his hand to the back of her head so he could take her neck with his mouth. Soft caresses turned hungry soon enough, his teeth scraping her flesh. Nibbles here and there elicited moans from deep in her chest. Lily reached up, gripped the god's arms, and pulled him forward. He didn't actually come forward with her efforts because he was a big thing and hard for her to move. However, Boreas took her not-so-subtle hint and stepped closer so they were body on body and she felt his warmth all down her front while he sucked at the sensitive valley where her neck met her shoulder. She gasped at the delicious drag of his fangs across her skin, and Boreas let out a rumbling groan in response.

Her body heated, ached, filled with want and need in equal measure, and she wouldn't wait any longer. She twisted out of his single-handed grip, managing to get a small amount of space between them in the process, and moved toward the shower. Reaching in without looking, she blindly felt for the lever that jumpstarted her shower. "You joining me?" she called to the god, who she might call frozen in place if not for the hard rise and fall of his chest and the flicker of light in his eyes.

Lily then started to strip. The process lacked seduction, or at least seductive intent. Undressing was necessary to get what she wanted – Boreas inside of her – so she did it as quickly as possible. When she straightened, after pulling her leggings and panties off at the same time and flicking off her socks, Boreas also stood fully naked in front of her.

The cave had plenty of light, sure. She'd seen all Boreas had to offer. Still, something about the brilliant white of the bathroom walls and tile and the white lights around her mirror, washing the room in an abundance of light, made him all more focused and clearer. And delicious.

Boreas stared back, lost in his own thoughts, as she took her fill of him. In the small space, his pine and winter wind scent mixed with the steam starting to rise from the shower, making it more pronounced. His chiseled chest looked like one of those marble Greek statues she saw the one time she went to The Met in New York City. Except his bronze skin moved with his heavy breaths and had a smattering of white hair stretching across the massive expanse. Her eyes dragged down, searching for where she knew the white hair began again, right at the deep v below his thick, defined abs.

Her breath hitched. It was beautiful in ways she'd never thought a penis could be. It almost looked carved, like from a block of ice. The raised white swoops and swirls of the cyclone made her mouth water. When Boreas's hand came into sight and he gripped it tight at the base, her knees nearly buckled.

She dropped to her knees, partially to keep from accidentally doing so, but mainly to touch him, feel him, grab a little taste of him before she lost her mind. He seemed to know what she wanted, or maybe he just also wanted it. Boreas gripped the back of her head and guided her to his cock. Filled with desire and a need to taste, Lily let herself be guided, clasped her mouth firmly around him, and took him deep in one fell swoop.

Boreas let out a low moan that reverberated around the bathroom and gripped her head tighter, his claws snagging on the hair around her temples. Lily moaned herself, as the fresh, sweet taste of him, like snow cream made from the first big winter storm, overwhelmed her.

Her tongue traced the raised ridges, a weaker pleasure than when she had felt them inside her earlier, but a pleasure all the same. She went down deep, sucked hard, and his answering curse in another language sent a zip of satisfaction through her. Her focus stayed on him, his pleasure, which made her feel pleased as punch herself.

She managed to make about six strokes up and down before a growl ripped up the god's throat and he stepped back enough for his dick to pop free from her mouth. At superhuman speed, he had her up off the floor, the curtain to her shower ripped back, and both of them under the hot spray. Well, he stood under the hot spray and she managed to get secondary splashes. His wings took up a good amount of space even in her larger than average shower.

Thoughts of wings and showers went out of her head when her back hit the far end of the shower. Boreas loomed, devouring her with his icy eyes. His lip curled, a fang popping out, and it made her shiver. She hoped he'd use it on her, but he didn't. Not then. Instead, his magic filled the space, sending an ice-cold wind to whip in a very focused manner, right at her nipples.

Lily's back arched and she let out a yelp at the wonderful, surprise sting of it. Her peaks pebbled, hard and needy, and when she thought she couldn't take any more of the cold, focused wind on her skin, Boreas replaced it with his mouth, instantly heating her to her core. She gripped the back of his head and held him tightly to her. His tongue and his fangs worked a different type of magic, lathing and scraping and soothing all together.

She whimpered in disappointment when he tore himself away. "I need you," he said, and it had the sound of a true confession, of a pious worshipper on their knees before their own deity. Lily moaned out, "Now," and without preamble, Boreas notched his gloriously ridged penis to her pussy and pushed deep.

They groaned in unison, and he paused for a moment before he started to pump. There was no pause, no easing into a pace. He took her, hard and fast, her back slamming into the cold tile and her legs locked tight around his strong waist. The sharp feathers of his wings tickled her feet but she ignored it, didn't need to for long. The feel of his ridged cock deep inside of her, dragging in and out in quick hard thrusts, overtook all other sensations quickly. Until her orgasm bubbled to the surface, coming fast and strong, ripping a scream from her throat as she clasped down hard on him deep inside her, urging him to stay there. Possibly forever.

He grunted but kept up, hoisting her into a higher position on the wall and somehow going faster, deeper, harder into her. "One more," he grunted out, pinning her mouth to his with a fierce, demanding kiss.

She didn't know if she could give him another orgasm, but after a few minutes, he moved a claw down to circle her throbbing clit, and she shattered under him without warning, like a glass ornament falling from a Christmas tree, all jagged, sharp sparkles on the floor. Lily felt him tense, buck, and he shuddered hard inside her and she knew he found his own release. He still held her to the wall, his weight on her a comfort. Then he slowly eased out, a loss she felt in her core, as he kissed her shoulder with quick pecks. "Let us clean you up," he said, moving slightly so the warm water finally cascaded over her skin.

Boreas fed her cold cuts, cheese, and crackers with his hands after he toweled her dry and plied her with water from her jug filter. Filled to the brim with food and water and good orgasms, she snuggled into his arms on her bed. "If you need to go," she began to say but he hushed her with a claw to her lips.

"May I stay?"

She smiled at him. "Of course. Let's get comfy." They burrowed deep under her covers, both still naked, and hugged tight as sleep took her. She slept soundly until she felt soft kisses peppering her face.

Streaks of gray winter dawn lit the bedroom as Lily's eyes opened, and Boreas, in all his winged glory, hovered above her. "I must go. Much to do today," he said, though he did not clarify what a god did all day. She sleepily thought she should ask him sometime.

He stroked her face with a single claw and asked, "Would you go to dinner with me this evening?"

"Like a date?"

"Yes," he confirmed, and for some absurd reason, he looked nervous.

"Of course. What time?"

"I'll meet you at your shop when you close for the night."

"It's a date," she mumbled, shifting back into the covers to get at least a few more minutes of sleep. She felt another kiss to her cheek, heard the rustle of sharp feathers, and knew Boreas left before she drifted back into a dreamless rest.

Chapter 14

"Aren't you going to do something with those brows?" Isa asked, arching her own in the process.

Lily'd been busy adjusting her fleece tights under her green babydoll dress, but at Isa's remark she let out of huff of fake affront. "What exactly would you suggest?"

"Have any brow gel?" Isa asked.

She shook her head no, but Isa rummaged around in the small makeup bag on the bathroom counter, looking to see what surprises she might uncover. Lily had lots of makeup because she liked it. It was fun to try new things, even if she often wore the same minimal bits on a daily basis.

"Aha!" Isa said in triumph, pulling out her brown mascara. When Lily reached for it, Isa slapped her hand away. "I got it," she said, turning her boss's chin her way and swiping the mascara across Lily's brows in soft strokes.

"Just a little bit..." Isa said, concentrating on her task as Lily fretted. "Perfection," Isa declared as she stepped back to admire her work.

Lily snorted but Isa narrowed her eyes. "None of that, Lily. You're looking fabulous and don't think otherwise."

It wasn't like Lily disliked her looks, but maybe she was nervous about the date. Why, she couldn't comprehend, given the fact she'd been in lots of compromising positions with Boreas already. Still, nerves fluttered in her belly.

"Thinks for the help, Isa," she said, scooping up the remnants of makeup on the bathroom sink. "You can go ahead and head out if you want."

"What if I want to meet your man? Ask about his intentions?"

Lily shooed her out of the small bathroom space and toward the back. "Go on. Get. You have choir practice anyway."

"True, which is the only reason I'm leaving." She blew Lily a kiss and laughed as she glided out the backdoor, leaving infectious teenage joy in her wake. Something Lily appreciated in the moment as it calmed her odd nerves a bit.

She'd shut everything down a few minutes early to have time to get ready and figuratively twiddled her thumbs as she waited for Boreas to show. A gentle tap on the glass of the front door made Lily whip her head around. She found Boreas there, smiling at her as he leaned against the window of her front display. Heat instantly rolled through her body at the sight. She noted, with sadness, his hands looked like human hands, not the more monstrous claws, but she brushed it aside, knowing he needed to hide his true form if they were going to be out in public. She didn't like the idea, but she understood it.

Beyond that, however, he looked glorious. His broad, open face held a slight smile just for her. The ice in his eyes melted when their gazes connected. His hair, tied back as usual, shone bright white in the fading light of the evening.

He wore a fine leather jacket, the deep brown worn with age. Underneath, she caught glimpses of a red and green plaid shirt, a bit of early Christmas encasing those lovely muscles she wanted to trace with her tongue. His legs were clad in dark, loose-fitting denim that still stretched tight over his hard thighs. He wore big brown hiking boots, hiding his feet. It wasn't the full, delicious display of his usual toga, but he looked good enough to take a bite out of, nonetheless.

His eyes mesmerized her, and without thought, she started toward her mate. Her mate. Odd, but she felt the truth of it deep in her bones.

When she unlocked the front door and swung it open, Boreas moved her back into the depths of the store and quickly shut it behind him. "Hello," he whispered, taking in the outfit she'd obsessed over for the few minutes she had to do so that morning.

"Hi," she replied, shy now in the face of him. She lowered her gaze, seeing their feet so close, boots to boots. She felt a finger, not tipped in a claw, snag her chin and lift her face. When their eyes met again, he searched her, like he could see into her mind and found something he liked. He bent down and planted a soft, quick kiss to her lips.

"Hello," he said again, as if he'd forgotten he'd said it, and she laughed. He followed suit with a deep husky chuckle, and the trance they had been in dissipated.

"We've done that already," she said, turning to walk back to her counter, where she snatched up her puffer coat, hat, and gloves as well as the small wristlet she carried in her big coat pockets in the winter instead of a shoulder bag. "So, where are we off to? Should we head to my car?" She hooked her thumb toward the back but he shook his head.

"No. We are staying close." Boreas took her coat and helped her slip it on. She donned her gloves before he placed the hat on her head, giving the top an affectionate tap when he had it snugly in place.

She figured she knew where they were headed, but she put her arm in his offered elbow and said, "Lead the way, then," as they exited out the front. They paused for her to lock up and walked the three blocks up to the one restaurant in downtown Holly Hollow. Hickory stood at the end of the row of shops, a small farm-to-table spot known for smoked meats and a rustic vibe.

It'd been a while since she'd been in, but she knew the owners well. Much like she knew all the people in Holly Hollows and particularly anyone who had a business in the downtown area. The hostess, their waitress, and the chef/owner who came from the back all waved Lily's way and gave her warm greetings. When they were placed at a small table for two in the back corner of the place, Boreas arched a brow at her in question.

"Small town livin'," she answered to his unasked question and he huffed like he understood.

"Like Olympus," he said as he studied the drink menu in front of him.

The oddity of this, the differences between them, hit her full force. Of course he was a god, she knew this full well. But that also meant there were other gods, maybe from all types of pantheons. Possibly all over the place.

"So you hang with the Greek set. Are there also Egyptian and Norse and Japanese and Aztec sets?"

He acted as if he would speak but paused before he began. The waitress appeared a second later, ready to take the drink orders (a winter ale for him and a glass of the house red for her). Lily gave a quick suggestion of food, so they went ahead and ordered that, too. The corn fritters as an appetizer and the smoked meat plate to share, which Hickory touted as enough for two, but in Lily's experience, seemed more like enough for four. Once the waitress took their order and retreated, Boreas answered her question.

"Basically."

No elaboration. "Why did humans turn on you gods back in the day?"

Boreas shook his head then sighed. "Many gods did many, many things wrong in their time. They ruled too harshly. When humans rebelled, the majority of each pantheon moved into the shadows, happy to lick their wounds and be relegated to mythology. Some still flit around your world, living alongside humans. Undetected."

"You were one of those outside-the-world sorts?"

He nodded. "I had no reason to engage with humanity."

"Until I twisted my ankle in your stomping grounds," she chirped.

A deep chuckle again, music to her ears. "Exactly," he said. "No purpose until you came along."

They locked eyes again, and the rest of the restaurant fell away for a moment. Nothing existed but them, the connection she felt to him in her gut, and the seconds stretched between them.

However, the spell broke when the waitress set their drinks down in front of them. Lily blushed as Boreas thanked the young woman and things went back to normal-date territory.

She learned what he did with his time, which mainly consisted of studying, keeping tabs on his three wind brothers and the smattering of gods he still contacted, and making sure all stayed right in his little section of forest. He apparently also dabbled in the stock market with the help of his old friend Plutus, had since its inception, so he made money the semi-old-fashioned way.

Boreas asked her questions, too. About her granny and her brother. Asked how she got into candle-making. She told him how she loved it as a teenager, moved away from it as a graphic design major in college, but came back to it when she couldn't do quite enough freelancing to pay all her bills. Lily's Lights started small but boomed pretty quick. "Thanks in part to you," she added at the end, raising her glass to him in a quasi-toast.

"Glad to help."

"I'm sure you are." She didn't need to see Ryan to know the voice interrupting their conversation. He stood there, a smug look firm on his face though slightly tattered at the edges, as if it might unravel at any moment. Madison hung on his arm, looking unbothered by anyone and anything. Above it all, apparently.

Boreas rose from his seat and Ryan visibly flinched, though he pulled his face back into his annoyed scowl quickly enough. Lily pressed her hand into the god's chest to try to calm him as she looked Ryan up and down. "You should leave," she said.

Madison tugged slightly on Ryan's arm and said, "Our table is this way, babe." She still looked unbothered, but for the first time, Lily noticed the shuffling of her feet, and the way her eyes darted around the room when no one looked directly at her face. Something to think on more later, but not when her mate and her ex might have a brawl in the middle of Hickory.

"Leaving sounds better," Boreas rumbled. Lily tapped her hand on his chest. He closed one of his over it and gripped it tight, keeping it connected to him as he stared down her ex.

"Oh, I don't know. We planned on a nice, romantic date. Right, Madison?" Ryan looked cool, but Lily'd seen his reaction to Boreas, who, even in human form, outmatched him in height and bulk by enough to make any dude who might want to start some nonsense hesitate. The smart move would be to go. Maybe even run, given the strain on Boreas's face right then.

Madison looked between the two men, then at Lily, and asked "What's the deal here?"

"No deal, hun. Really. Nothing for you to worry your pretty little head over," Ryan said, patting her like a child and using that infuriating, condescending tone Lily knew too well. "In fact, why don't we join you? Hey Kathy," He called the waitress over. "Can we add a table here?"

Lily managed to shake her head at the young lady who gave her apologies to Ryan and said something about clear walkways and fire codes.

"Oh, well then. Another time." He stared right at Boreas and repeated himself. "Another time."

Boreas stewed, but he said nothing as Ryan and Madison took a table in the opposite corner. Ryan stared between Lily and the god, ignoring Madison, who appeared to be scrolling on her phone – when she wasn't sending questioning looks Lily's way.

"Kathy?" Lily called. When she came over she asked, low, "Can we get our food to go?"

"Sure thing," Kathy said, worry and relief warring on her face. Like most service workers, she didn't need or want customers' personal issues bleeding all over her floor.

She came back a few minutes later with to go containers and thanked them for coming in. Lily tossed cash on the table, enough to cover the meal and a large, well-deserved tip. Boreas grumbled something about it but she shot him a look. "Let's just go." Without another word, but plenty of death glares over at Ryan, Boreas helped her into her coat again and escorted her out the door, putting a far too quick end to their first real date.

Boreas seethed the entire ride to Lily's house. Seething might be an exaggeration for an average man, but not Boreas. He was a god. Boreas said nothing, but his breath came out in chilly bursts that fogged up Lily's windshield. When she told him to knock it off so she could see, his breathing calmed some, but a small layer of ice formed along his hairline, eyebrows, and lashes. He literally sat in a cold fury.

Lily understood it, to some extent. Ryan continued to be the same annoying ass she'd had to deal with for a good chunk of her life. Of course she understood. She couldn't understand the intensity of his reaction in the moment, though, or why, exactly icy anger swirled around him.

As soon as they were both over the threshold of her house, Boreas reached into the front of his shirt and fished out a small metal pendant on a cord. It hung so low on his neck she hadn't noticed it. As soon as he whipped it over his head, his features blurred then sharpened, turning him back into the Boreas she knew, the monstrous god she'd originally met.

"Handy necklace." She hung her coat up in her foyer and bent to unzip her boots. His large claws gripped her waist tight as she bent over a second before she moved, as if propelled by air, her boot dangling off a toe for a split second then hitting her living room floor with a thud. "Hey, now. I was in the middle of something."

Boreas wasn't listening. He deposited her butt right on her dining room table and growled "Wait. Here." The strength of his voice, the intensity of his gaze left her breathless, so she merely nodded her head as he stormed off, presumably checking the house for gods knew what. When he came back after his recon mission, his eyes were no less intense.

"All good?"

"No. All is not 'good.'" He flexed his jaw so hard Lily expected one of those fangs to snap right off. Luckily, that didn't happen.

"Hey. Hey." She called to him, reaching up to place a comforting hand on his chest. "You okay?"

"No." Deep, hard breaths, then he continued. "I must take care of this Ryan."

"What do you mean 'take care of'?" She had no love for Ryan, but the anger pulsing off Boreas in cold waves and her love of old mafia movies made her stick on the phrasing.

"He will not bother you again."

"Look, Boreas. He's an ass, that's for certain. He quite possibly deserves a takedown of some kind, but what you seem to be suggesting is a little too far."

He arched a white eyebrow her way and she noticed the ice had melted, leaving small droplets of water on his lashes. She decided a direct approach might be in order: "You cannot kill him." She quickly added, "Or smite him."

"Why not?" He sounded like a pouty kid, but Lily ignored the petulance.

"Because it's wrong to kill someone when you're not directly defending yourself."

"I am defending you."

"Not from immediate physical harm," she countered, scooting closer to him, her butt now sitting precariously on the edge of the table.

"You are mine to protect," he said, shooting hands out to grip her shoulders tight. "Mine."

"Is this a mate thing?"

Boreas huffed out a laugh. "Yes and no. Ryan is a threat, albeit not a physical threat so far. Any threat should be eliminated. However, when someone is threatening another's mate..." He trailed off.

Lily got it on some level. The idea of Boreas in trouble or in pain made her gut twist and her anger rise. Because he was used to lording over things as a god, and because he was her mate, he needed to protect her. His need also stirred something primal in her, and she hitched up her legs slightly to hook them around his hips. His hands instantly moved to the outside of her thighs, to secure her. To rub her.

"Lily," he ground out, turning his head away. "It might not be safe for you at this moment. I may– I do not know if I can control myself after what transpired this evening."

"Then don't," she replied, caressing his chest as it rose and fell in sharp breaths. "I'm yours, ain't I? Maybe making me yours in another way would help calm you down."

"If we do this now, Lily, I won't be able to hold back. I will take you."

She looked up into his blue eyes flashing white with their now crinkled edges. He worried for her. Always did, which was why he'd been so pissed about Ryan. He also worried he'd hurt her. Always had, which was why he'd hesitated to connect with her for so long. Something in him feared what he'd do to her. But she had no such fear.

"I'm yours. You're mine. There's nothing you could do to truly hurt me besides leaving me alone, without you. There's nothing to take I wouldn't freely give." Lily placed one of his hands on her chest, over her heart. She didn't say the words, but she felt them there already. Sent the feeling down the tie that bound them heart to heart.

A different growl, low and fierce and needy, left Boreas as he gently pushed her chest back until she lay sprawled on her dining room table. Lily looked up into his glowing eyes, his fanged mouth open in a snarl of want, his wings spread wide behind him. "You. Are. Mine." Each word seared into her, a promise she felt all the way to her bones, just as she felt his claws move down to flip up her dress.

She heard a tearing sound, though she didn't feel the claws. She did feel cold air brush against her exposed pussy. He must have ripped right through her fleece-lined leggings and panties both. "Mine," he growled once again before he knelt between her legs. His massive hands spread her wide, exposed her to his gaze. She went up on her elbows to see what he was doing. He stared intently at her core, then looked to her face as he blew an icy stream across her. She shivered, from cold and want, and he gave a predatory smile as he parted her with a single thumb and flicked her clit with a claw. "Mine."

She moaned at his touch, then screamed when he dove forward, giving her slit a long, lingering lick from bottom to top. Little coherent thought crossed her mind afterward. She became only feeling. The scrape of his slightly rough tongue, the pinch of his fangs, the grip of his claws on her inner thighs wrecked her. He worked her core expertly, licking and sucking and groaning all the while, as if it brought him pleasure.

After a few minutes of his groans and her moans, his licks and sucks, he said, "Come for me," before lashing his tongue at impossible speed across her clit. The hard, quick lapping at her already primed clit made her come in record time, the sensation running riot in her blood. Lily let out a harsh cry and lifted off the table as she clamped her thighs tight around the still kneeling Boreas, unable to control her body.

Boreas appeared above her, hovering, his wings sending a gentle breeze across the room. He leaned in, kissing her fiercely, and she tasted them both on his tongue. Ripping himself away with a soft curse, he gripped her waist and dragged her back down the table. She didn't know if she could stand, but he forced her to; he flipped her around, her belly hitting the hard wood of the table.

He hitched her hips higher, so high she almost had to go up on tiptoes to alleviate the stress. Boreas's body stretched across her back and his tongue hit her ear, licking and sucking for a moment. A quick nip of his fangs brought a yelp of surprise from Lily though it didn't really hurt. "I am taking what is mine," he whispered to her, and her body bucked at the words.

The god, still fully dressed, straightened and she heard the quick slide of his zipper before she felt the nudge of his cock against her entrance.

He wasted no time. Boreas slammed into her, hard enough to take her breath, and lingered for a moment so she felt the scrape of his jeans against the back of her thighs. His claws dug into the dress high on her hips and she had a single stray thought about how it would likely rip. However, all thoughts faded when he pulled back out. Every ridge and rise of his dick tickled her insides and she relished the feel even as she wanted him to fill her up once again. The god did not make her wait. He slammed back home, ground hard against her ass, and started a punishing pace.

The room filled with the sounds of flesh slapping flesh, deep groans from Boreas, and rising screams of pleasure from Lily. She couldn't control herself and didn't want to. Didn't need to. Boreas wanted all of her, every bit of flesh and pleasure and feeling. As his perfectly ribbed cock slid in and out of her, he adjusted so he knocked perfectly against the spot deep inside her that made her go feral. She began clawing at the table and she would've left deep gouges if she had Boreas's hands.

She clawed not to get away, but for purchase. She wanted to fuck him back, leverage herself so she could slam back into him harder and faster. What he did to her, as he bore hard and deep into her pussy, reaching farther than anyone ever had before. A claiming she thought they'd already experienced. Boreas obviously needed it to calm himself after their confrontation at Hickory. What Lily hadn't realized was she needed it as well. Wanted to be claimed by this brilliant, protective, thoughtful god.

Boreas picked up pace somehow and Lily gave another cry. Still, she heard his deep groan. "Give it to me, my flower. Give it to me once again."

The words, the slide and thrust of him, the grip of his claws on her, all merged into a brilliant, shimmering moment of pure sensation, an answer to the achy need she'd felt since meeting Boreas. She screamed out his name as he called out her own, and they came together, panting and moaning and slowing their pace only because their bodies forced them to do so. The orgasm roared inside her, thrumming hard against the bond she felt with the god, so hard, in fact, she sensed a strengthening in their connection, like a chain wrapping around a taut rope.

After a beat and a huff of breath, Boreas lay on top of her. He squished her slightly against the table but she didn't mind. Especially when he laced his hand on top of hers. She turned her head to see them, human hand under massive, clawed hand, and he gave her a sweet, lingering kiss on her exposed cheek. Lily wouldn't of course, but she thought she might like to stay just like that for forever.

Chapter 15

Lily noticed a delicious soreness to her core as she bent across one of her corner display tables to add more candles. The deep pinch brought sensations from the previous night to her mind. Which, in turn, brought heat to her cheeks and a sly smile to her face. The smile died a quick death, however, when she spun from the display and saw Madison standing at her front door.

The woman had yet to knock, but she sure as hell saw Lily look her way. She gave a silent gesture for Lily to open the door. With a sigh, Lily walked that way, dreading whatever snark might be on Madison's morning agenda given what happened the night before. Still, she was raised right, so she let the woman in out of the freezing cold morning.

Madison stomped her feet on the welcome mat inside the door as she shivered. "It's colder than a well-digger's behind out there."

Lily made an affirmative noise but stood waiting in silence, letting Madison get to whatever she needed to say so early in the morning.

"How you doing today?" Madison asked, and Lily noticed her rubbing her hands together not for warmth now, but in a nervous jiggle.

"It's early, Madison, and I still need to get my prep work done before I open. Can I help you with something?"

Madison huffed out some air and looked Lily up and down. "Last night was...odd." Lily snorted a laugh, and Madison powered through. "Yeah. Odd. And after you and the big guy left, it got... odder."

"How so?"

Madison brushed a stray hair from her face and straightened, as if preparing herself. "I didn't start dating Ryan or anything, just so you know. Last night was the first time we went out."

"Okay..."

"Well, we flirted, okay? I knew the stories. Heard the warning you gave. I just--I didn't think *I* needed to worry, you know?"

That sounded more like the usual Madison so Lily nodded along.

"Anyway, after the Christmas Masquerade, he asked me out. He's cute. Has good money. He's from a good family. Why wouldn't I say yes?"

"Because I told you."

Another loud huff of air. "Yep. You sure did. I didn't listen."

"What happened, Madison?" Lily suddenly thought maybe something bad happened to Madison the night before, and the fear of it made her reach out for the other woman's hand. "Did he hurt you?"

"Oh, no. No. Nothing like that. Scared the shit out of me, sure, but he didn't lay hands to me or anything. He got all fired up after the confrontation y'all had at Hickory. Talked about nothing else the whole night and kept calling that goodlooking guy you were with dangerous." Lily swallowed a lump in her throat at that little tidbit, but bit her tongue so she could get the full story. "We had drinks, dinner. The whole time, he talked about nothing but you. How he needed to save you."

"That sounds annoying," Lily said, trying to empathize, but Madison stopped her with a hand.

"Sure as hell was, but that's not the half of it, Lily. He rushed us through eating and got me back to his car. From there he drove us not to my house, but to yours."

"What?" Lily whispered.

"Yeah. It was jacked." Madison shook her head at the memory, but kept going. "I called him on it, said he was behaving like a stalker or something, but he acted like I wasn't even there. Like he pushed out anything that wasn't about you. He parked up on the wide shoulder along O'Bryan's Curve then got out and tracked down to your place without his car. He came back after about twenty minutes looking fit to be tied, muttering again about you being in danger and drove back down to town like a maniac. I couldn't get out of his car fast enough when he dropped me off."

Madison gripped her hand tight and looked deep into her eyes. Lily saw the regret reflected there before she even spoke again. "I should've called you last night when he left me in the car by your place, but I don't know, I felt weird and stupid and scared of what he might do if he found out."

"Madison, don't take that on your head. You can't control him, and you shouldn't try. Also smart to make yourself safe before you did anything else. The important thing is you came and told me first thing, and I appreciate that. No need to be down on yourself."

"No, there is lots of need. I've been too lost in my own selfishness and judgements for too long. Time for me to grow up and stop being the same mean girl who ran roughshod in Holly Hollow High. Last night shook me up a bit, had me up thinking through a lot of things."

"Madison, you've always been good–"

"For your business, yes. I'm good at my job and help people who pay me to do so, but I tend to be nasty in other ways. A lot like Ryan, actually, which is what made me start thinking hard on it."

"You were never as bad as Ryan," Lily tried to reassure, but the woman let her hands slip away and waved them in the air.

"I was stuck in a certain attitude and Ryan shook me loose from it. Can't say I'll change overnight, but I'll try. First thing first? This. Warning you to keep an eye on Ryan and let you know what he did. I for sure wouldn't want him skulking around my place in the dead of night."

"I sure do appreciate it, Madison. It's a good start, for you and for us." Lily offered her hand again, in a handshake. Madison stared at it a moment then took it, firm and quick, before giving a megawatt smile.

"Enough about the dirtbag Ryan. Now that we're friends and all, you wanna tell me about your new man?"

Lily barked out a laugh. "I'll hold off on that for now, Madison." She didn't add that she wouldn't be telling Madison any deep secrets anytime soon. The woman might be on a road to change, but Lily wasn't about to test drive on it.

"Fair enough. The way he looked at Ryan and took care of you last night, I'd say I'll be seeing more of him around anyway."

"Sure hope so," Lily muttered.

"Me, too." Madison whispered. When she caught Lily's gaze, she gave a firm nod. "I mean it, Lily. You need anything, let me know. You want to go to the law about Ryan, I'm happy to serve as a witness."

"You sure about that?"

A bit of the old Madison came through in the look that fell across her face. "That man deserves nothing less, and I'd like to help you give it to him."

Okay, then. Seemed definitive on her end. "In the meantime, you need anything–"

"I'm good," Madison waved her hand toward the door. "Need to get going, start my own workday."

"Again, thanks a lot, Madison."

Madison bundled herself back as tight as she could, and said her goodbyes as she swept back out the front door. Lily watched her walk down the street to her car. She'd gotten up early to tell Lily this, to warn her, and in the cold of winter in Holly Hollow. The woman walked the same, eating the sidewalk with each step, firm and sure of herself. Maybe she wanted to become a new Madison, and Lily hoped so. For Madison's sake.

She bit her lip, thinking on things. What Madison told her and Ryan's increased obsession. She needed to talk to Boreas about it more seriously, and soon. They needed a plan, and quick. She didn't want this ruining her Christmas when it now looked so bright in so many other ways.

Thinking on that, she slipped back on her coat, let herself out the front quickly and relocked it, before she shuffled to meet with Mitch down the block. She'd be opening a few minutes late, but it'd be worth it, come Christmas Day.

"And I said to him, I said, 'Now look here, Ralph. You're acting like you ain't got a lick of sense. We've been doing business this way for decades, ain't no reason to change it up now just because you saw some random video on the Facebooks."

Lily tried to hide her smile at Betty's rant. They both had a lull in business, and the older woman had taken the opportunity to come chat with her friend about her husband's "tomfoolery" as she called it. She gave Betty her ear, nodded, ohed and uh-huhed when necessary, and tamped down her laugh. The older woman huffed and puffed in anger, but Lily knew it was really more annoyance than anything else. Getting it out made her sweet as pie for her husband after they had their little disagreements. She was happy to lend the ear Betty needed.

The tinkle of her front doorbell sounded and Betty stopped her rant to look over her shoulder and see who entered. Lily didn't need to do so, because as soon as the first note struck, she also felt the soft stroke of wind and smelled the pine and cold scent she'd come to love.

"Oh, now, look at that," Betty said, and Lily figured she spoke about Boreas, who she watched enter the shop in long, sure strides. When she looked to her friend, however, Betty studied Lily's face, not the door. She cocked her head and Betty twirled a knobby finger a few inches from her nose. "That there is the look of someone plum smitten."

Lily couldn't deny being smitten with her godly mate, so she just chuckled and moved from around the counter to meet Boreas halfway. He bent down slightly to land a sweet kiss to the top of her head as he put his large, firm hands to her hips and gave them a gentle squeeze.

"Hi," he said, close to her face, his breath sweeping over her in a gentle breeze.

"Hi," she echoed, the smile she felt stretched across her face coming through loud in clear in her tone as well.

A throat cleared behind them and Boreas's icy eyes crinkled in amusement when Betty started. "Good to see you again, young man."

He stepped around but swung Lily's arm into his own so she came face to face with Betty at his side. "You as well, Mrs. Booth. How are you today?"

Betty waved her hand, "Fair to middling, I suppose. Would be better if my Ralph listened to me more. Or maybe looked like you. Not that he wasn't a looker himself back in the day, mind. Age gets the best of us all."

Lily giggled but slapped her hand over her mouth to rein it in. Boreas shifted on his feet, as if Betty's words made the god uncomfortable. Or maybe the intense gaze she swept over him had him twitching.

"You sticking around then?" She asked as Lily tugged his arm and they moved from the center of the floor back toward the sales counter.

Boreas looked down at her a beat and said, without looking away, "Of course."

"Good." Betty clapped her hands and said, "You got plans for Christmas Day? Lily, and her brother when he's in town, usually come by mine for dinner. You're welcome to join."

"Oh, no, Betty, we don't want to impose," Lily said.

"Psshht. Ain't no imposition. The more the merrier, they say, and we all want to have a Merry Christmas. Right?"

Boreas looked like a beast frozen by the sharp gaze of a predator, the way he wide-eyed Betty at her direct question. Lily decided to put him out of his misery. "We'll let you know, Betty. Okay?"

"Sure, sure. Don't wait too long, though. Gotta go pick up the ham from Edgar's Farm and want one big enough for everybody."

"Will do," Lily promised.

"Welp, seeing as it's about lunch, and this man seems to have something for you two, I'll leave you both to it. Try to go talk Ralph out of more foolishness." The older woman shuffled toward the door and Boreas laid down the brown paper sack in his hand before hurrying to open the door before she reached it.

"Why thank you, young man," Betty said, giving him a maternal pat on his arm as she left.

Before he could speak, Lily said, "Betty's a bit of a firecracker. Something you might need to get used to if you are sticking around."

In a flash, he popped up beside her, folding her into his warm arms and leaning in close. He didn't reply to her words. Instead, he brushed a stray strand of hair off her face and dove in for a quick, searing kiss she felt all the way down to her toes. She may have still been a little wobbly when he righted her and moved to unpack the sack he had with him.

Lily watched as he brought out fresh sandwiches from the deli down the street and two bags of chips. Only half-thinking, she asked, "Is it weird for you, not having your claws when you're in human disguise?"

"No. It is simply another form of me."

Lily reached over, taking his hand in hers and tracing the veins there. It looked an awful lot like his godly hand, but slightly smaller and without the clawed tips. She brought his finger to her mouth and gave it a kiss. "Well, I miss the claws. And the wings. They're so pretty."

Boreas didn't answer, and she looked up to find his ice-blue eyes blazing white. "Lily," he growled out and she felt heat pooling at his look and tone. He grabbed her up again, holding her tighter than before, and gave her a hungry, roving kiss that lasted a few minutes. Luckily, no one came through the front door as he used his lips on hers to tell her exactly what he wanted to do with her.

When he finally broke away, he set her bottom on her stool and pulled it closer to the corner of the counter, where he distributed the lunches. He stood beside where she sat and gently unwrapped his own sandwich as she continued to stare at hers in a daze.

"Eat," he said, firm command in his voice.

"You want me to eat, you shouldn't kiss me like that right before you set a sandwich in front of me," she quipped. However, she managed to shake herself out of her lust fog and start her food. "Thanks, by the way."

Boreas gave some masculine sound she took to mean a combination of "you're welcome" and "no big deal" and left it at that. She unwrapped what turned out to be a warm chicken panini. "Madison came by this morning before I opened."

He arched a perfect white brow in question as he took a bite of his sandwich.

"Madison and I have a complicated relationship. Well, more like Madison has a complicated relationship with a lot of people in this town. That may change, though, after what happened last night."

Boreas set his sandwich down and stared at her, waiting for more info. "Seems Ryan ranted a whole lot about you being dangerous. He drove her out to my house, left her in the car, and went snooping while we were home last night. Together." She didn't need to say what they were doing as they both likely remembered it vividly. Lily sure as heck knew she wouldn't look at her dining room table the same ever again.

"Thank you for telling me," he said, then went back to his sandwich. As if she hadn't just told him Ryan may have pulled a peeping Tom act on them last night.

"Boreas, he could've–" Seen him rip off his spell necklace. Seen them having sex on her kitchen table. Both not things she'd want him to see.

Boreas stopped her worry spiral quickly. "No, he could not," he said around mouthful of panini. "I warded your home after I found the camera in your carport. He would not be able to see anything or get within ten feet of your house."

"You didn't think to tell me about that?"

"You did not ask."

"How'm I supposed to ask about magical stuff I don't even know is possible? Like, what even is a ward anyway?"

He wiped his mouth with a brown paper napkin and explained. "A ward is a simple spell, usually used to repel certain people or groups from a specific location."

"Okay. Straightforward enough. How'd you cast it?"

"I told you I can perform basic spells. Wards are basic spells."

"Okay. Still. Doesn't explain why you didn't tell me."

"I would have, Lily. It happened only two nights ago. A lot of other things have transpired since. I was not purposefully keeping it from you or magically monitoring you. I am not Ryan."

The itch Lily'd felt along her skin at the mention of him doing something to her house eased. She hadn't even realized the issue, but he had. She had a bad taste left from Ryan's shenanigans. But, as he said, Boreas was not Ryan. She knew this. "Sorry," she muttered, looking down at her cooling sandwich.

A warm finger stroked her cheek, and she lifted her gaze to meet Boreas's. "You do not owe me an apology. Your history makes you hesitant about such things, which is reasonable. I should have told you as soon as I did it, but I have been distracted. For that, I apologize."

She grabbed his hand at her cheek and gave it another swift kiss as she held it. "You're nothing like him. I hope you know I know that."

He nodded and went back to eating. Lily decided to drop the conversation. They'd talk more if Ryan made a move against them again. Just then, she wanted to focus on tasty food, her luscious god, and teasing conversation that ended with them both hot and ready. Sadly, no afternoon delight occurred. Lily did agree to meet him on the gravel road close to his cave that evening. She assumed delight would be had then, which she could hardly wait to savor.

Chapter 16

Lily got used to the cave bathroom setup in quick order and had even brought a little on-the-go bag with her last night. Meant she could snuggle in bed longer with Boreas, cocooned in his scent and feathers, before heading out for the day. Also meant some good morning fondling and panting in his big shower, which she did not mind at all.

When she'd thrown her pink gloss on and tossed it in her bag, she turned to her god and said, "All done." He scooped her up like he loved to do, the Superman hold he used so well, and started toward her car.

The wind whipped around them, but a soft layer of warmth enveloped her, and she couldn't tell if Boreas's body heat or his magic caused it. Didn't matter. Not really. All of it felt snug and right. But she wondered something.

"Why like this?" she asked.

He looked down at her, one perfect white brow arched. She wiggled her butt and his eyes narrowed, gripping her tighter.

"Do not do that," he growled out.

"Okay, okay. Probably not too smart, I'll give you that. Just meant to ask why you carry me like this."

"How else should I carry you?"

Valid question, Lily thought, as she considered the logistics of the matter.

"I could hold onto your waist, lay against your front? Might be more aerodynamic."

The ice in his eyes flashed white and she knew he'd thought something naughty. The idea of what they could do in the sky sent shivers up and down her back.

"Not secure enough," he said with a gruff finality.

Maybe true. Maybe not. Or maybe, she thought, she could get him to try something new and bring out whatever sexy thought crossed his mind. Something to look forward to in the future. Possibly when it wasn't so damn cold out.

Lily snuggled back into his chest, taking comfort in his warm embrace. So much so, the thump of Boreas's feet landing on the ground jolted her eyes open. She'd closed them at some point in their journey but she couldn't remember when.

He pulled her closer, into his chest in a brief hug before he bent and allowed her to stand from his arms. She did so, though her body hesitated when she stepped away from him.

"Look at that, safe and sound," she chirped as she checked her phone. "Plenty of time to grab a coffee before I open the shop."

"Is today your last day before your break?" he asked.

"No. Like most businesses downtown, I stay open half a day on Christmas Eve for all those last-minute shoppers. Then I'll have a glorious vacation for a whole week."

"Would you like to go somewhere?"

"Like where?"

Boreas reached up to cup her cheek and smiled down at her. "Anywhere you wish to go, my flower."

Not for the first time, she thought there were lots of perks to being with a god. Then she thought of him flying them off to some tropical location and she burst out laughing at the stray old joke.

"What's so funny?"

"Just flew in from Appalachia, and boy, are my wings tired," she said in her best old-timey comic voice. He stared at her and she shook the unasked question away. "Just an old joke setup that might be true for you. Not important."

He shrugged it off and said, "We can get away if you wish. However you wish to do so."

Lily grabbed the front folds of his toga and pulled him in close. "No need to get away. All I want is a week in bed with you."

He growled, deep and sexy, before he said, "More than happy to oblige such a wish."

"But"—she stepped away toward her car—"we can't be in bed all day on Christmas. You already had me confirm with Betty, and there'd be hell to pay if we don't show at her place for dinner when you said we would."

He nodded then she asked. "What are your plans for today?"

He twirled a hand in the air. "I have a few important calls and inquiries to make."

"Oh la-dee-da. Mr. Fancy Pants but without the pants," she teased.

Before she could blink, he pinned her against the car. Her heart pounded, but not in fear, despite his wicked sharp claws, massive size, and inhuman speed. Never in fear of this monster she might just come to love. Might already love.

He grinned down at her, gripped her chin so his claws gave a delicious scrape against her skin, and tilted her head toward him. He took her mouth, hard and rough and delicious, before he stepped away.

"Be safe, my flower. I will see you this evening?"

"Yep. Come by my place. I'm feeling like spending time with a Christmas tree and watching a Christmas movie." She was in the holiday spirit and he didn't have anything like that in his cave.

With jerk of his head in agreement, Boreas took off, leaving Lily to climb into her car and wait a few minutes for it to warm up and defrost before she left.

About three miles away, after the gravel road turned into a narrow asphalt lane, Lily slammed on the brakes. In the middle of the road, stretched clean across it so she couldn't get around without stopping, sat a shiny new luxury car. Ryan leaned against the gleaming white vehicle, looking pleased with himself. She had no time for his mess, and she knew Boreas flew behind her somewhere, so she muttered a few choice cuss words to herself and put the car in reverse, hoping to catch her god and avoid whatever mess Ryan wanted to throw at her.

Ryan held his hand up, as if that would stop her. Lily rolled down her window, to yell as she pulled away, when he called out, "I have proof of what he is."

Again, Lily slammed on the brakes. Her heart pounded, and her knuckles turned white on the steering wheel. She didn't reply, but she also didn't continue backing away as Ryan strolled toward her. She stared at the cold road, mind whirling over how much Ryan might know and how he might know it.

When he reached her car, he leaned down, folding his elbow on the open window so he took up all of her vision when she turned her head his way. A photo dangled between two fingers. She snatched it up, studying the grainy image: Boreas, in all his monstrous god glory, clawed hand held high in the air and sharply feathered wings spread wide. It was the day after their first night together. When he made the snow dance for her. A sweet moment now made sour by Ryan's intrusion.

For a beat, Lily was confused by how he even intruded, then she remembered. The camera, of course. The one Boreas found minutes later, after Ryan's angry call. Sadly, he didn't find it before it captured this. Lily cursed herself under her breath for not thinking of this, not realizing Ryan knew all along. She'd been so happy, even with the annoyance of her ex, so warm in her little mate bubble with Boreas, the consequences of the camera being there never fully registered.

"This is just a screenshot, of course. It's a whole video. You were all giggly over his little snow trick, but I doubt others will be." He paused, looked at her with pity in his eyes, and said, "He's a monster, Lil."

"You have no idea who he is." The venom in her voice lashed out because she couldn't, but with a man like Ryan, it didn't really hit.

"You're right. I don't know specifics. I also don't care. He took what was mine, and I'll have it back."

"You're talking about me, you know. A person. Not a thing."

"It's a monster, Lily," repeated with more bite.

"*He* is a living, breathing, feeling being. And one I wouldn't fuck with if I were you."

Ryan shook his head. "I'm thinking, if he doesn't usually look like this when he's out and about, he has good reason to hide it from people. Here's what I'll do: I'll destroy the video if he leaves. If he doesn't, I'll expose him to the whole town."

"Why are you like this?" How could she ever have loved this man? Because she *had* loved him once. She'd been too blinded by it to see who he was really, and that fact haunted her sometimes. Especially when he behaved like a little shit.

" I want him gone, off to whatever rock he crawled out from under. And I want you back. "

"You can force him out, I guess, but you can't force me to be with you."

"We'll see," he said, and his hand shot out to touch her face. She whipped her head as far away from his reach as she could, but she couldn't go far with the seatbelt and all. He managed to touch a wisp of her hair and she felt sick at the feel of him so close.

He straightened and walked back to his car. Before he got in, he yelled out. "He has until tomorrow, Lil, or the whole town will know there's a monster in those woods, not some white bear from their stories."

He revved his engine as he righted his sedan and drove away, leaving Lily breathing heavy. She felt heated, confused, and the chilly wind blowing through her still open window didn't help. She didn't know what might help, if anything. But she had to warn Boreas.

She didn't want to think about what he might do. If he might leave. Secrecy had been important to him and she'd known that from the start. He deserved to know his true form might no longer be so secret, and he deserved to make his own choice on the matter. Even if his choice might break her heart.

Lily couldn't lie. Well, she could about small things, like when she lied to her granny about breaking her favorite pie plate and said the cat knocked it off the counter. She couldn't lie about the big things. They showed all over her face. Which is what Boreas saw as soon as she opened the door to her little house later that night.

"What's wrong?" He pushed her into the house and swiftly closed the door.

For her part, she also didn't beat around the bush. "Ryan knows."

"Knows what?"

"Well, he knows you're not human. Not the specifics, like you're the God of the North Wind, but he knows enough."

Boreas stiffened and ground out, "Tell me."

She did. Told him every detail, down to his glowing eyes in the picture and the clarity of his sharp teeth and glistening wings. When she repeated Ryan's threat and demands, Boreas stiffened, but said nothing for far too long.

"Boreas?" She needed to know what to do, what to think, if he planned to leave and break her heart.

"Yes?"

"He knows you aren't human."

"And?"

"He could expose you."

"And?"

She started at that. "You were real worried about exposure not too long ago. Seemed to be one of the big reasons you didn't want to start things up with me."

"I most certainly have started things with you now."

She nodded.

"Lily, my flower. My mate. When I decided to be with you, to adhere to my purpose, you became my sole concern. If he exposes me, he exposes me. I have ways to mitigate any action he may take."

"But—"

"No buts, sweet Lily. I am a god of old. I can handle a man throwing a tantrum."

He wrapped her up in a strong hug a touch too hard. Maybe a little desperate even. "Do not worry, Lily. I will see to Ryan."

"Are you... Will you..." She couldn't even bring herself to say it out loud, but he still knew what she wished to ask.

"I am not giving you up, Lily. Never."

"But he'll--"

"He will do nothing. I will take care of it."

"Like, take care of him?" She asked. Ryan was an ass, but she wasn't sure she could fully condone murder. He cocked his head in question and Lily mimicked slitting someone's throat.

"As satisfying as that might be, such actions are not exactly acceptable in this age. I have other avenues open to me. Ones which will lead us to a better future."

"What avenues?"

He hugged her again and stepped back. Back towards the door as he reached for the doorknob. He was leaving, which made her blood race despite his assurances.

"I will explain all soon enough, but time is of the essence. Sadly, I must leave to handle this situation."

"You're not *leaving* leaving, right?" He'd left her without word or promise of his return before. He hadn't done so since the masquerade, and they'd worked through his initial hesitancy, but the pain of not knowing what he might do or think or where he might go made her more than a little nervous.

He stepped back into her, gripped her hands, and looked deep into her eyes. "I know what I did, what I said before, may make you hesitate now, my flower. Please, do trust me. Trust us now."

Lily gave him the benefit of the doubt. Sure, she worried, but she needed to let him handle things, especially things dealing with godhood, magic, and his choices.

She took a deep breath in and out through her nose. "Okay," she whispered, giving him a good squeeze back. Then he gave her a hot, short kiss and in a rush of wind the door closed on him, the lingering smell of winter wind and pine the only thing left.

Chapter 17

Worry stalked her steps as she paced her shop around noon the next day. Granny'd drilled into her the old adage "don't go borrowing worry," but she felt pretty damn sure now was a time to worry. Boreas never returned. He went off gods knew where doing what she supposed gods did when they were being blackmailed. On top of that, Ryan had given a clear deadline for today.

She wouldn't give into his demands. That wasn't close to happening, consequences be damned. She wouldn't give up her freedom, her sanity, her body for another. Boreas also wouldn't want that for her. He might leave, had left in the past even if he always returned, but she knew, in the place where their bond stitched itself to her soul, he'd never do anything to hurt her, physically or emotionally. He couldn't. Just as she knew she couldn't do anything to hurt him. Still, life had a way of ripping through happiness, and she worried their bond might be shredded in the process.

Three whole customers had come through that morning, each in a last-minute-gift rush, so she'd had plenty of time and space to keep this level of fretting going strong. A sigh rose out of her chest, and she checked her phone for the nine hundredth time in an hour. Only 11:42. Eighteen minutes to close and forever before she'd know the fate of her relationship. Pessimistic thoughts for sure, but her thoughts nonetheless.

Suddenly, a boom sounded, like a plane hitting super speed above them. A sonic boom, which she'd not heard often in Appalachia, far from any military base. Hell, they were hours away from a regular airport. Then a scream, long and terrified. It started faint, as if coming from far off, and got louder and louder, a speeding train of sound coming right toward her.

No, not a speeding train. A plane. A god, in fact, landing in the middle of the street, right in front of her shop. Boreas stood strong, his knees barely bending to take the brunt of the landing, a ghost-white Ryan wriggling in his outstretched hand like a dangling trash bag. Ryan's scream died seconds after landing, but his angry hysterics picked right up where the screams of terror left off.

"See? See everyone? He's a monster! He's not human!" He wiggled more violently, but he might as well have been a kitten caught by the scruff. The god stood stoic and tall, letting Ryan scream his fool head off about monsters and safety and what-about-the-children nonsense. Slowly, one by one, business doors swung open around her, and her friends, her neighbors, her townsfolk started to file out into the street.

Lily rushed out herself, not as hesitant as the others, only stopping a few feet away from Boreas because she'd rather not get too close to the frantic Ryan. When she stilled, Boreas let the man go, throwing him onto the dirty street where Lily figured he kind of belonged. The god then crossed his arms, and Lily took in the meaning of the sight in front of her. Boreas had flown into the middle of the downtown Holly Hollow business district in the cold of winter, wings sharp and gleaming in the gray winter light. His claws splayed across his bulging arms, and the sneer on his lips showed off his elongated canines to full effect. His clawed toes tapped the ground because he wore no shoes, only the toga he favored when not out in public.

But he was. Very much out in public. On full display for the whole damn town to see.

"What are you doing?" Lily asked, hushed and worried.

Before Boreas could answer, Ryan, still on his knees, shuffled over to her and gripped the front of her denim apron. "Lily, run! You're not safe. None of us are safe from this thing!" The ass was laying it on thick, intentionally, to try to rile up the town.

She literally brushed him aside. Not a second too late, because Ryan putting his hands on her had Boreas out of his stoic stance, massive hands fisted and a clear growl ripping through the air.

She asked again, "What are you doing?"

Boreas's flippant answer: "Attempting not to kill this foolish man."

A snort had her snapping her head around to find Betty standing there, arms crossed and a hate-stare clear on her face. Not directed at Boreas or her, though. She stared daggers at Ryan. "Don't go stopping on our account."

A nervous laugh bubbled up and Lily couldn't keep it in. "But you--you're—." She gestured to all that was him out in the open.

Boreas nodded then reached out a clawed hand to bring her into his embrace. The warmth, the smell, the proximity of him calmed her. Then she remembered to trust him, and to feel the rush of relief at the fact he'd come back to her.

Without preamble, Boreas spoke, his gruff voice carrying to all the spectators gawking at the scene unfolding in the middle of Main Street. "I am Boreas, God of the North Wind. I have resided in your woods for many years, and I believe some of you caught glimpses of something you could not explain there. Now, I come to you as I am. In my true form. To ask you to accept me as one of your own."

Lily gripped the fine silky white of his toga, her breath caught in her ribcage, as she waited.

Betty spoke first. "Ppsshht. You were a part of us once you danced with our Lily at the masquerade. Anyone with eyes could see you were gone for her, and we love our girl."

Isa was there, too, somehow. She must have been out and about running errands or something, because she hadn't worked that day. "Yeah, my dude. No worries."

Lily, of course, still had all the worries.

Madison stepped up. She came closer, stepping around Ryan and giving him a mean girl look that translated clearly to "You're nothing but some worthless piece of dirt I don't want anywhere near my designer boots." She walked up to Lily and Boreas. Betty clucked her tongue, warming it up to give Madison hell if she said something out of line to Lily, but there was no need. "I like him for you. Looks like he took out the trash, too. I say he has a place here as long as he wants one."

"That'll be a long while," Boreas said, a grin finally stretching across his broad face, his teeth flashing.

"Anyone got a problem with this?" Madison called, turning in a circle to stare down every other person on the street. Lily didn't exactly go for intimidation tactics, but for this cause, she'd let Madison do her thing.

"I do!" Ryan yelled, finally on his feet. He reached to snatch Lily's hand, but Boreas acted quickly, bringing her several steps out of his reach in a heartbeat. "Careful," he warned. "I let you live after all you have done, but my patience grows thin."

"What's he done?" A man's voice carried the question, and Lily turned to make sure she had it right: it was Mitch, the silver worker who owned the jewelry store down the way. He frowned at Ryan.

"Noth–" Ryan began to say but Betty cut him off.

"The fool harassed Lily ever since he got back to town, that's what. Caught him myself a time or two being handsy in her shop." Betty spoke clear, Ralph at her back as always.

"He came in and started trouble with the two of them at my place the other night," Archie, the owner of Hickory added, looking at Ryan with a disgusted sneer.

"Yep," Madison said with a pop of her lips. "He stalked her. Even went to her house late at night to spy on her."

"He called, too. Like, all the time," Isa added, standing next to Madison in solidarity, a sight Lily never thought she'd see.

"No. It's not like that," Ryan said, whatever lie he had packed away tripping over his tongue before he could get it out.

"He placed cameras on her property," Boreas said to a round of gasps. No one liked the other stuff, sure, but one thing you did not do in Appalachia was mess with someone else's property. Big no-no there.

"He's a monster," Ryan screamed, waving his hands at Boreas. "He kidnapped me, put me in a dangerous situation to fly me here. Lily must be saved."

"Yeah, from you," Isa said, with a snort. "Looks like Boreas did just that. Plus, he ain't no worse than the vamps who come to shop or the werewolves roaming around Western Kentucky. Get over yourself, bro."

The circle of people, which now included the sheriff Lily'd known her whole life, closed in on their smaller group. Ryan smiled at the sheriff, "Thank God someone is listening."

"Oh, we've all been listening." Mitch had apparently become the town spokesperson at some point. "Listening to how you've harassed Lily, how this young man helped her, and maybe taught you a lesson you needed teaching."

Boreas snorted at 'young man'. He'd likely never get away from it here, despite his centuries and centuries of age.

Still looking at the Sheriff, Ryan asked, "Aren't you going to do something?"

"What would you like me to do? Throw harassment charges at you?"

In the face of his failed plan, Ryan turned to something else to get his way. "He kidnapped me."

"I didn't see anything like that," Betty sniffed. Murmurs of agreement went up all around.

"He's a monster."

"The only monster here is you, Ryan," Lily said, holding onto Boreas tight. Looking around at the people she'd known most, if not all, of her life, she didn't see hate or fear directed at Boreas. She saw assessing looks, sure. The type any good Appalachian gave a newcomer. But no sneers his way. Ryan, on the other hand, got more than a handful of dirty looks.

"I'm thinking it might be best you go. Not back to your office or your mama's place. Go on out of town," the sheriff said. Not to Boreas, but to Ryan.

A laugh from Betty broke the tension. "Not like you'll get any business here now anyways."

"Y'all are crazy. Every single one of you," Ryan screeched as he turned in a circle.

"No. We protect our own, like Lily. Like this new fella."

"I was born and raised here" he gritted out, hands clinched into tight fists he couldn't sue in this crowd.

"May be. But you ain't one of us. Not the way you've acted." Mitch's voice spit venom with those words.

Ryan looked dumbstruck. He muttered, stuttered, but couldn't get out any more arguments. Not very lawyerly of him, but when one faced a bunch of pillars of a small community telling you off, it'd likely do your head in. Seeing he had no allies, no foothold, he cut everyone a withering glare and stomped away.

"I'm calling his mama. Tell her what a fool he just made of himself." Stella, the antique store owner, hurried away, clutching her Christmas cardigan to herself. Others muttered introductions, shook Boreas's clawed hands, had kind words for him and Lily both, but they soon dispersed. It was Christmas Eve after all, and past noon at this point. Everyone wanted to close up and get on home.

Betty, however, lingered, looking Boreas up and down. "You that white bear everyone's been ranting about, huh? I can see it."

"Betty..." Lily hesitated, the question she wanted, needed to ask stuck for a minute.

"Yeah, hun?"

"Um, why don't you care? You know? About--" she waved at all his godly glory. She appreciated it, sure, but no one else seemed even a little bit fazed by it.

"Lily dear, this is Appalachia. We know all kinds of things stalk those woods and hills and hollows. Nice to meet one of them in the flesh finally." She patted Boreas on his bare arms and dismissed the concern. "What I want to know is if y'all are still coming to dinner tomorrow night after all this mess." It wasn't a question, not really, and Lily knew it.

So did Boreas apparently. "Yes, ma'am."

Betty clapped her hands together in delight. "Whoo doggies, I'm going to have you at my table first. All the ladies at church will be green with envy."

Lily laughed at Betty's words, at the questioning, hawkish tilt to Boreas's head, at the way her community showed up for her. Showed her love. She found a lot to be joyful about in that moment, and Lily wasn't about to let it pass without sending that joy back out into the world, to twirl on the winter winds.

After Betty finally left them alone so she could close for the day, Lily dragged Boreas into the shop, locked the front door behind them, then sagged against it. "That sure was something," she muttered.

Boreas didn't reply. He pinned her in place, massive arms on either side of her head, and bent to give her a kiss. It sizzled on her lips, the spark and flare of her desire meeting his in a flash of want and need. She whined when he pulled away too quickly, but she had pressing questions that made her shake it clear just as quick.

"What happened out there?"

"I showed myself to the town in order to expose Ryan."

"Um, yeah. You sure did that. What about your exposure issues?"

He waved a hand in the air. "No longer a concern."

"Not good enough, Boreas," she said, a hard edge to her voice as she cocked out a hip.

He chuckled at her. Chuckled! Then twirled her around, pushing her all the way to the back counter. "I visited Hecate last night. Acquired a certain charm to help make sure my secret could be open in this town but not leave the confines of it. People here can talk of it here to people from here, but not anywhere else."

"Most wouldn't."

"I believe you're right. Ryan would, might even be trying to do so as we speak, but he'll find himself unable."

"It was just a geography issue? Keeping it contained?"

Boreas pulled her close so they were only a breath away. "No, my flower. I once dreaded what your town would do, but no longer. I learned more of you, your friends, and guessed the reaction would not be as bad as it could be. More so, I needed to do it. For you. My purpose. My love."

"Your love?" Lily's voice cracked on the question and Boreas moved a claw up to trace the outline of her ear as he pushed back some of her brown hair.

"You. My love."

A gasping sob left her, like something had been bottled up and came unstopped suddenly. "I love you," she managed to croak out around the swell of emotion.

Boreas held her tight, bringing her up so he could give her a sweet but heated kiss. A loving kiss, Lily realized.

When the embrace ended, she asked "Any other surprises for today?"

"Today I believe we may have had enough."

Lily agreed, and found herself bouncing through closing, happy to hop into Boreas's cozy arms when she finished up and head to his cave for the night. He loved her and she loved him. They were mated. He had no more reason to hide. It was Christmas Eve. All was calm and bright in her small world.

Chapter 18

With the cat out of the bag so to speak, Boreas scooped her up tight in his arms as he so loved to do and flew her away from the shop, straight to his cave. The freedom of it–the chilly winds encompassing her like an embrace as she rested comfortable and safe in Boreas's strong, warm arms and watching the snowy tops of pine trees pass below them like a sparrow on the wind–coursed through her veins. Part of it could've been the freedom of those she loved knowing who and what Boreas was, of them siding with her against Ryan. The warmth of support and care from all those around her, including the god maneuvering them through his cave, caused tears to prick her eyes.

When he set her down, Boreas noticed. Reaching up to catch a stray tear before it fell, he asked, "Are you well, my flower?"

"I am now. More than ever, actually." Then, she jumped him. Quite literally. Without warning, Lily gave a little hop into the air, clamping her arms around his shoulders and her legs around his waist. He caught her easily, as she suspected he always would from here on out.

Her god gripped her ass and held her close, a growl leaving his lips as he searched for hers. The kiss seared. Cleansed. Cleared away the worry and stress and left only the twang of longing and the euphoria of love in its wake. Lily moaned into his mouth, taking the time to trace his knife-like incisor with the tip of her tongue. She'd never feared them, never feared him in a physical sense. She'd feared not having this. However, her fear stayed firmly in the past, and all she saw in her future was a life with this kind, gruff, lovely god holding her.

She tore her lips away. "Say it again," she whispered as she peppered his lust-filled face with kisses. The white light haze of his icy eyes focused on her in question a few seconds before he got what she wanted.

"I love you, my flower. You are my purpose."

She gave another quick, hot kiss at the words then pulled back to say, "The best Christmas present a girl could ask for."

His deep masculine chuckle shook them both. "We'll see if we can do a little better than that." A second later, she sailed through the air, thrown from across the room to land with a soft thump on the comfy platform bed in the far corner. Before she could right herself, Boreas hovered over her, one thick claw slicing down her sweater.

"I like this sweater!" She said in protest, but there was little heat in her words and a laugh in her voice. By the god, she'd never been so giddy and happy in the arms of a man before.

"I will find you a dozen more," he said with the flick of his wrist, exposing her torso to his cool gaze. He dipped a hand into her bra and pulled one breast free before he sent a chilly wind over the nipple to make it pebble. She shuddered with cold and anticipation as he followed behind his wind, taking the peaked tip into his mouth and sucking hard. A whimper preceded a deep groan, then the sound of lust and longing and the sound of flesh on flesh filled the space

Pine filled her nose, so sharp and lovely she couldn't think clearly around it as she reached for a handful of his white hair and gave a sharp tug. "Boreas," she moaned, wanting more but unable to articulate it.

He heard something that spurred him on, as he made quick work of both their clothes. Instead of entering her with his throbbing, swirling cock, he rolled them over to place her above him. "Ride me," he demanded before giving her control.

Lily reached between them to grip him in her fist. A pump, up and down, brought a hiss to his lips. She focused on the feel of the swirling ridges along his length, on the way they snagged the skin of her palm and how delicious she knew they felt when he moved inside her.

Without much thought other than what lay in her hands and the pleasure ahead, she lifted her hips, notched Boreas at her entrance, then slid down at a steady pace. The god threw back his head beneath her, the veins in his neck bulging as his blue-white eyes closed tight. It was the look of ecstasy, and Lily drank it down deep, just as she took him deep inside herself.

His eyes popped open, roving over her face, her body, the place where they connected. He gripped her hips tight then helped her grind down hard on him. "Damn, you feel so good," he huffed out between hard breaths.

She lost herself, pumping her hips up and down, focusing on the delicious slide of his cock and the look of pure adoration in his eyes. "I love you, Boreas," she moaned, echoing what she'd said earlier.

A tension snapped and he curled up, meeting her mouth with nips of his teeth. His hands took on more work, moving her with lightning-fast speed on top of him. His groans and growls poured into her like refreshing water, nourishing her very soul. She wrapped her arms tight around his shoulders, held on for the ride, and came with a deep moan of his name. Seconds later, he followed, pumping his seed into her as he whispered words of love, over and over again.

After long, silent minutes with only their breath mingling in the bed, Lily looked up from where she lay on his chest. His eyes were already on her. With a smirk, she said, "That might just have been a better Christmas present."

The god laughed, big and joyful, and sweet, pine-scented wind whipped around them in a happy breeze. Lily snuggled down, falling asleep to the feel of his warm body, his chilly wind, and the love they now wrapped around them like armor.

She must've been dead to the world, because after their amazing romp, the next thing she knew, she awoke hours later in an empty bed . Not an empty cave, however. Boreas sat in his leather chair, staring at a Christmas tree he hadn't had the afternoon before.

Lily rubbed her eyes awake and in a sleep-thick voice asked, "What time is it?"

She heard the smile in his voice when he said, "Three in the morning."

"Merry Christmas, then," she chirped back.

Suddenly, the god scooped her up. She laughed. "I can walk, you know."

He shrugged it off. "Why should you, when I am perfectly happy to carry you?"

Still wrapped in his blanket and now wrapped in his arms, she didn't argue the point, and let him position her on his lap. On the side table, he had two steaming cups of hot chocolate and two large muffins all ready for them. "Mmm-huh. Cranberry orange. My favorite," she said around a big old bite.

"Betty may have told me. In fact, she may have forced these upon me."

Sounded an awful lot like something Betty would do.

They ate and drank in companionable silence, the occasional slurp of cocoa or clearing of a throat all the noise they made. Lily laid on his chest, warm and content, long after she finished her tasty treat, and stared at the Christmas tree.

It looked like a forest pine he'd plucked straight from the ground, and it likely was. There were a few shiny ornaments here and there, some bits of holly woven throughout, and some real snow he somehow made cling to the branches. Under it sat a small red box. A gift for her, she presumed, but she wanted to beat him to it.

Boreas tried to grip her tight as she twisted free, but she managed to get loose. The blanket trailed behind her as she wrapped it around her body like a robe and went to her purse, where she pulled out a small, oblong box wrapped in snow-white paper with a tiny silver ribbon in one corner.

"Merry Christmas," she repeated, beyond happy with herself.

"You intentionally did this," he pouted.

"What? Buy you a Christmas present? Well duh. You kind of have to be intentional when you do something like that."

Instead of taking his present in hand, he took up her body and repositioned them as he had before. He sent a wind whipping around, and the red box plopped down between them. "Merry Christmas," he said, a sly grin on his face.

She held his present out to him and shook it in his face, because by the god she'd said it first, so he had to open first. He sighed but took it, carefully slicing the wrapping open with his claw. The box looked tiny in his monstrous hand, but he used the utmost care in opening it. When he finally plucked the gift free, it glinted in the low light of the fireplace. It was a silver bookmark etched with pine trees and swirls of wind.

Boreas stared for a long moment without saying anything and Lily rushed to explain. "It's real silver, hammered down and etched by a jeweler in town. I had him do the pines and wind, because, well, that's what you smell like to me. Pines and cold wind."

"It's perfect," he said, pulling her forward into a rough hug. "Thank you my flower."

Happy with his reaction, she preened for a moment until he set his bookmark down and offered her her gift. "Open."

"So bossy." She wasn't as neat as him in peeling away the bright red paper, but she sure slowed when she saw a ring box underneath. Delicately, she turned the box over before resting it in her palm. She creaked the lid open and saw a massive diamond ring nestled in black velvet.

"What?" she asked, even though she very clearly could see what it was.

Boreas took the ring from her palm and looked deep into her eyes. "We are mates, my love. It is a bond unbroken. However, you are also human, and there are other important bonds you observe." He pulled the ring from its place and offered it to her between his clawed thumb and forefinger. "Lily, will you marry me?"

Blood pumped in her ears and she stayed speechless for long enough Boreas started to squirm under her lap. She blinked away her shock and surprise then and gushed out, "Yes. Of course I'll marry you, Boreas."

He slipped the ring on her finger. The large, princess cut diamond flanked by two large oval sapphires twinkled in the fire light. The silver band had etchings similar to his bookmark along the sides. She looked up at him in surprise. "We went to the same jeweler," he said, a wide smile on his face.

There was nothing to say, nothing to do except kiss the god she loved and hold him tight to her. She'd had lots of great Christmas mornings in her life, thanks to the love of her family, but this one topped them all. "Best Christmas ever," she whispered against his lips.

"Good, but we can make it better. Again. We have many hours before Betty expects us at her home."

"Oh, she'll love this," Lily said, admiring her ring as he carried her back to his bed. Their bed. "And she'll be ornery as all hell if we're late and have this kind of news, so we can't get too carried away."

He looked at her with serious eyes. "You carried me away long ago."

She sighed into the kisses he peppered on her lips before he moved over her face. Boreas scraped a sharp fang across her cheek and a smile bloomed. She wasn't lying when she called it the best Christmas ever. Lily suspected, however, there would be loads of best Christmases in their future. Better and better Christmases, filled with love, friends, and beautiful candles lighting their way.

Please take a moment to rate *Chilly Little Thing* on Goodreads!

Want More?

Want to see who the Book of Desire goes after next? Be sure to keep an eye on my website for my next release!

To get awesome travel and cat pics and first looks at all her books (and any freebies she might have in the works), join her newsletter over on Substack.

For news and the occasional laugh, follow Sonya Lawson on social media. She's @sonyalawson on TikTok, Instagram, and Facebook. Get all new book notifications by following her author profiles on Goodreads and BookBub, too.

You can find all things Sonya Lawson on her website at sonyalawson.com and her Books page lists all her current publications.

And, once again, please take a moment to rate/review *Chilly Little Thing* on Goodreads and/or wherever you purchased this book. All honest reviews are greatly appreciated!

About the Author

Sonya Lawson is a recovering academic who now writes romance (in a wide variety of sub-genres). Her work offers a glimpse into different yet familiar worlds that are sometimes dark, sometimes dramatic, sometimes a funny, and always steamy.

While she remains a rural Kentuckian at heart, she currently ives in the Pacific Northwest. Her days are often filled with writing, editing, reading, and walking old forests.

You can keep up to date with all her happenings by following her on social media (TikTok, Instagram, or Facebook) via her handle @sonyalawsonwrites. If you join her Substack newsletter, also sonyalawsonwrites, you'll get early access to news and hot deals.

Acknowledgements

The idea for this book popped into my head rather suddenly. Because it's a holiday book, I had to work double-time to get some of the things that go into a good indie book done. Of course, lots of people helped along the way, and this book wouldn't be out and about if it wasn't for them.

Dayna Hart of Heart to Heart to Hart Edits came in clutch on this one. It's my first time working with her as an editor and she gave such helpful feedback. She also has an eagle eye for style and grammar. All things I needed. Big thanks to her for the great work she did on this novel.

I used an amazing artist for my cover and she nailed it. Gisele (lifebygisa on Insta incase you want to see more) understood my vision better than I did. I often have a hard time expressing things visually, so her help and guidance really made this cover come to life. Thank you so much for the time and artistry you put into this adorable cover. I love it more and more every day.

I added new people to my ARC team for this book because I was starting a new genre. So much thanks and appreciation go to those ARC readers (old and brand new) for taking a chance on an indie writer.

The monster romance groups I'm a part of on Discord really helped out with both finding new ARC team members and getting the word out on this book. Monster romance readers are truly the best, y'all. Thanks!

This book wouldn't be what it is without specific input and help from Kenzie Kelly. She's a fellow monster romance writer who gave great feedback and helped me promote along the way. I love batting ideas around with her and look forward to reading her next monster book very soon. (And if you haven't yet, you should go read her first monster romance – Held by a Monster).

Kassie Keegan, who has her own beastly alien creations in her Savage Planet series, also gave me space in her Facebook group to promote my ARC sign up and my book in general. She's a great writer and an amazing human being I'm lucky to call friend.

On a related note, I can't thank A.R., B.Z., Karri, Kassie, Kenzie, and Nicole enough for being the loveliest writing group around. Their care, concern, writer minds, business savvy, and encouragement boost all my writing days. I couldn't do this with quite so much focus and confidence if not for them.

As always, my friends and family pull me through when writing or life days are dark. Thanks for the constant and unwavering support, loves.

Last, I need to thank all the people out there who work to make this world safe for writers like me to express their ideas and share their words without negative consequences. This might change in the U.S. and it's not something that should change. I promise I'll do my damnedest to stop it from changing, and I hope anyone who's reading this right now will do the same.

Made in United States
Troutdale, OR
04/03/2025